DREAMS
OF A
BALL IN FLIGHT

STORIES FROM THE BOTTOM OF THE CUP

TIM FLOOD

UNDER RUNNING LAUGHTER BOOKS

Published by Under Running Laughter Press
1349 E. Ellis Dr., Tucson, AZ. 85719
www.dreamsofaballinflight.com

First published in the United States of America
by *Under Running Laughter Press, 2008*

3 5 7 9 10 8 6 4 2

PUBLISHER'S NOTE

ISBN 978-0-9797159-0-7

Printed in the United States of America by Lightning Source

Design and Layout by Catherine Craig
Cover Art by Joshua Kai Flood
Thanks to Jim Ricker for back cover photograph

For Miss Ever So Lovely

Tryshe

Who opens Windows

For Air
For Light
For Sound
For Love

CONTENTS

DREAMS OF A BALL IN FLIGHT

STORIES FROM THE BOTTOM OF THE CUP

Lucky Star

Anzio called to Denise with the distant sound of mortar and small arms fire. She smelled the acrid smoke as the landing craft hit the beach. The Captain waved the other doctors and nurses ashore. Here she was again, following the Rangers into another country in pursuit of the same war. North Africa had produced two long years of sun, sweat, grime and human gristle. Rommel's gift to the medical corps. She stood in shallow water and wiped her eyes. The Captain was already well up the beach. She strained to hear him.

"We are all midwives at the creation of the other..."

Denise shook her head. She thought she had heard a voice. Louise caught her shoulder. "You all right?"

Denise heaved, her upper lip revealing her toothy smile. "Sure, Lou, this is the way I always imagined it would be." Denise forced herself forward, up the high bank of sand.

The dirty canvas operating tent housed chaos. Stacks of gurneys held capacity loads of clients fresh from the front twenty miles north. It was always like something she had never seen and never wanted to see again.

She and Lou smoked Lucky Strike's sitting outside on the ground beside their hooch. The lines on their faces belied their twenty-one years. The night was still and the sky quiet. Denise could see the moon sparkle in Lou's necklace, made up of pieces of shrapnel taken from the bodies of the boys. Lou said she did it *"in memory,"* and neither of them thought it macabre.

"Captain wants to take us somewhere at dawn," said Denise.

"Us? I thought he only had his peepers on you," she said.

"I guess he knows that two are better than one."

"So, you accepted?"

"All I've ever done is to say yes, Lou." Denise stared off into the big night cave.

She remembered the family camping trips and how her father always said that the stars were campfires flung out across the void. She carried the peace and certainty of her father's voice in the bottom of her heart, yet longed for arrival at some inexplicable destination. The truth was that she couldn't wait and for what, she didn't know.

"Life must be built step by step..."

The jeep peeled out down the mud rut of a road, headed north.

The Captain sat in back with Denise, who turned up her lips at Lou sitting next to the handsome young Lieutenant who drove. The Captain had arranged for them to work the night shift.

"Where we going," said Lou.

The Captain leaned forward, putting his hand softly on Denise's knee.

"To Naples, I know a good seafood restaurant there."

Denise felt the warmth of his skin through her long john's. She wondered why it had taken him two years to touch her. She had worked so closely with him for so long that she knew what lay behind his every breath.

"Thought that was in Mussolini's hands," she said.

"No, we took it last night, let's celebrate."

Their jeep was sprayed with mud as they passed several convoys of boys returning from the front. The soldiers' grim faces remained in Denise's mind until the Lieutenant took the last hill into the town at full speed. They hit the cobblestones hard and gasped as the harbor came into view. The old town looked like it was a maze of smoked Swiss cheese. They turned under an old Roman portal and were met with heavy rifle fire. One round pierced the windshield as the driver spun out trying to break and turn around all at once. They crashed against an old wall. The engine died, but the Lieutenant managed to fire it up and the jeep jammed forward, back through the arch and out of town.

"Guess the Major had his facts mixed up," said the Captain.

"Guess so," said the Lieutenant.

Lou and Denise giggled and dug even deeper into their seats.

"Take that turnoff - there," said the Captain, when they were about halfway back, "We can't let them spoil a good day."

Vesuvius loomed. The still smoldering volcano blocked out the sky and held them in silence. They parked in a cinder field near a shabby blue sign that read, *Pompeii*. They walked down the streets of stone, buried in ash for seventeen hundred years. Wide-eyed they examined an intricate fountain, restored to reveal the artistry of the ancient Samnites who built the lavish port city.

"Look, over here," said Denise. She had strolled into the baths. The others entered and saw her standing over a body of ash which was frozen in a hard gray grimace of horror, grasping for the edge of the blue tiled spa. No one moved. Denise bowed her head in prayer.

"We are all just walking home..."

Outside, on the circular walls of the fountain, they drank the Captain's wine and saluted the hues of the setting Mediterranean sun, exhilarated by their escape from time.

They had been back at work for a few hours. They labored in the intensity of the stale tent and the immensity of their charge.

Denise heard the whistle and drone first. She dropped under the operating table as the bomb hit. It was a direct hit and the force of it blew her through the tent into the dawn sky towards the morning star.

Saki

Kern flipped the coin on her table, nodded with a rueful smile, coughed and banged out the door. He pounded up the boardwalk, past her sign that read "Saki, Clairvoyant – 25 cents" and wondered if the wrinkled old broad was right. He heard her words again,

"You are going to take a long trip in the spring."

Then he began to chuckle, which led to a full-blown bellow as he dodged the carts – hacked, spit and crossed over the dusty street into Minsky's for a drink.

Lunch Mouth nudged Ryan. "See that guy over in the corner, it's that pitcher, Dangerous Dan Kern, the one we saw play down in Philly last summer."

"You're full of crap," said Ryan.

"Oh, yeah! Take a look at that curly hair, and his eyes, I remember that look when he beaned Whitey Townsend, we was sittin right there behind the plate!"

Ryan turned for another look. Kern eyed him back, coughed wildly and took another slug of whiskey.

"I think you're right, Mouth, I do believe you're right, when the Athletics played the Mutuals."

Lunch Mouth headed up to the bar then circled around and slapped Kern on the back.

Kern lurched forward, his large gnarly hands hung on to his drink.

"What, what the hell you doin, mister!" Said Kern.

"No offense, Dangerous Dan, no offense, just wanted to let you know that you're the damnedest pitcher we ever did see," said Lunch Mouth as he plunked into a seat. Ryan followed suit, signaling for a bottle.

Kern sized them up, nothing much, hot air, no trouble.

"Well, thanks, but I don't have anything to do with it anymore, it's over."

"Whadya mean, Dan, the paper here says Mr. Spalding's gonna fire up an around the world exhibition trip in this comin summer of eighteen and eighty eight! Just three more months. Ain't no stoppin you from getting on with him, no sir, no goddamn way!"

"You won't know where you are then, until you know where you are now..."

Kern heard the seer's words again, blinked and stared at the big man as he rambled on about Kern's exploits with the round stitched ball. He heard about his own freak deliveries, the spitball, the emeryball and his use of licorice for instability and discoloration, to reduce visibility. "That's how he got that *Dangerous* moniker," Lunch Mouth assured Ryan. Kern drifted away with a nod to the boys.

"And your speed, Dan, your goddamn heater, jesus, you musta had them droolin outta their asses!" Lunch Mouth went on.

Kern just sat and saw his wife's eyes, saw the godawful glaze over them that said she was done. Done just like he was done now. Bankrupt like the league, infiltrated with gamblers and unpunished cheats, like the thoughts in his soul.

Kern stifled a yawn as the big yanker droned on. He had spent his whole life throwing a ball and wandering from town to town, a hired gun for whatever phony gentleman owned a team, an athletic roustabout, run out of hire, covered with the scurf of thirty-three years. The doctor gave him three more months, doomed by consumption, wracked by the wasted tissues.

"The score doesn't count and the 'best deal' is no deal at all..."

He thought again about her eyes, those deep eyes that once told him that he was the one, he was the one that counted. He vowed to go with what he had left in search of those blue eyes and a better day.

He froze up and coughed, coughed so violently that Lunch Mouth was silenced. He twisted up from the table and burst through the door of the saloon into the expanded light of spring.

Lying Dead

"While digging a footing for a set on the film, 'Borderman,' New Paradigm Production manager, Crystal Newman, notified authorities yesterday that her crew had unearthed what appeared to be some pioneer artifacts, next to the El Tiradito wishing shrine, south of downtown Tucson.

Professor Chas. Lyon examined the find. 'Remnants were found of an old leather pouch or carrying bag. Inside, there was a mineral or divining rod, a map, and some illegible legal papers,' Lyon said. The archaeologist indicated that the map was most certainly of an area south of the old mining town of Helvetia, on property currently controlled by Sidewinder Mines.

A spokesman for the mine said that the specific area had long since been worked and that the company was no longer actively mining there. He also said that the land was a late addition to the old Escalante land grant, known as the Huerfanos (Orphans) Float.

A local resident of the old Elysian Grove neighborhood, near the shrine, was interviewed during the commotion surrounding the discovery. Maria Oliveras said that she was upset about the filming and the 'desecration of the shrine.' She said that her grandmother brought her to the spot many times. 'Nana told me many stories about this place. My favorite was the story about an affair of the heart. She said that a child was born as a result of a tragic love triangle and that descendents of the child remain as keepers of the flame. I pray here everyday like I was taught...for the blessing of the fire...for a sense of the miraculous...and for the lying dead.' " (Old Pueblo Daily Star, 1998)

"Rattlesnake. You just ate rattlesnake flesh," Serafina said.

"What?" Said Nathan.

"I dug it out from under a rock, cut off its head, spliced it and marinated it in that sauce you like so well."

Nathan put his hand to his belly. He lay back and groaned.

For over a month, most of their hours were spent together. Nathan liked to watch her lithe body at work at the loom or sprawled upon the floor by the fireplace. He would reach for her as she passed him with her seductive stride, to hold her, to watch the flame of blood surge across her cheeks.

She would whisper to her friends in the pueblo about his powers with a mineral rod. In his hands, this magic stick moved in the direction of hidden silver and gold. They would play games. Nathan would hide his heavy gold pocket watch. Then he would place the rod in Serafina's hands and bid her to find it. It would refuse to move for her. He would take hold of her hand and show her how to grasp it in a gentle manner, to feel the energy passing. Still, it would not reveal.

After the shock of the meal, he asked her to play the game again. She was pulled by the bob and sway of the small cowhide wrap, hiding the secret vial of minerals at the end of the rod. She was pulled at last by her gut to the gold.

"It is like the hidden wind," she said.

Serafina rubbed the watch through her deft fingers.

Nathan's pleasure seemed to fade. *She has grasped my power.*

She saw him change. The watch fell from her hands, shattering the face on the red earthen tile below.

"You will be gone all day, again?" she said.

"And tonight," he said, " I've got to meet Della at her office in the morning and arrange the purchase of the land. Meet me at the Elysian Grove, Sunday, noon."

"Della, the *rubia*," she said, feeling him slip away.

"Strawberry blonde, she's the land agent."

"I know. Some say there's gold here," she said.

He put his finger to her lips, "Don't tell..."

She wrapped her palms on his neck and forced her eyes into him. He let go his resistance. They fell together, in soulful liquidity, breathing as one, in splendid dalliance. Her long black hair flowed across the threshold of the open door.

"In days gone by, some distance from the pueblo, there lived a beautiful senorita, whose hand was sought by two suitors. She could not decide between them, and in her desperation she found solace amid laced willows at the Elysian Grove and while there a mysterious hand struck her down. On this spot a shrine has been erected and every evening at twilight candles burn here, and people come by the hundreds to wish for what they want and it is said that they get what they wish for." (Anna Johnson, the Territorial, 1908)

Nathan slipped the mineral rod into the soft leather grip slung from his shoulder and mounted his lanky frame on the blue roan. Serafina held the reins. They noticed the young shepherd, Juan Oliveras, headed down through the mesquite bosque, towards the cottonwoods and the Rio Nuevo River. Serafina called to him. Juan turned and waved his sombrero. Nathan noticed the depth of her call, like a wolf calling her own.

Nathan Goodwin knew that the land held a secret, in the cirque enclosed by intersecting ridgelines on the east end of the property. His prospector grandfather's mineral rod had delivered him to the fissure in the escarpment, which revealed the lode. He had not told Serafina about the find and was amazed that she had guessed at it earlier.

He hadn't told her a lot of things. He had arranged for her to be returned to her parents in the morning. He had staked them for their desired return to Arizpe. His betrothed was due in town from Boston at noon on Sunday. Serafina would be well on her way to Mexico.

It was necessary for him to stop by the Escalante mine in order to collect the remainder of his required down payment. He rode northeast, up a spiny draw, past the twin pyramid hills known as the Huerfanos, under the building clouds of a stifling mid-summer sky, full of the moisture of an afternoon chubasco, up from the Sea of Cortez.

Serafina found the map to the cirque while cleaning the small adobe house. He had stashed it behind a retablo, one of the exquisite tin paintings he had bought below the border. Mentiroso! *Damn his lies and his secrets.* Nathan was not who he said he was. She felt her tummy and was glad she hadn't told him of her condition. Her mother had said, "He is not of your kind and does not know how to hold your heart."

Juan appeared outside the window. He reminded her of her first love, Estevan, who had been killed ten years before by revolutionary forces near Arizpe. She had fled north with her family to the Rio Nuevo River valley and the promise of fresh life. Through her craft she met many white pioneers, including Nathan when he purchased one of her intricately woven blankets. She had learned to be a weaver from the Indians near Rio Veso and added her own bright touches. It had provided for the family and enabled her to secure entrance into the territorial world of Arizona.

Juan tapped on the window. Serafina let him in.

"On account of the proximity of the excellent spring in the grove, many of the teamsters who drove freight wagons used to camp there. One such man drove a wagon between Magdelena and this place. He met a woman on the road one day who offered to sell him a map to a gold mine. He stole it and murdered her. At the camp, in the grove, he was heard bragging about his deed. A man searching the site for his beloved overheard the story. A fight ensued and the teamster killed this man also. The report got out that this man who was killed could perform miracles, and a great many people got the idea that if they placed a lighted candle here and prayed, they would get whatever it was they earnestly desired." (Cece Loveall, Old Pueblo Daily Star, 1927)

Simon Escalante thrust the coffee grounds from his mouth with his tongue.

"The Apaches have given this territory a bad name. Lucky you didn't have a mishap on the way over. Billy Sharp got axed by them last week down in the San Rafael valley - took his wife away, too. How's your little Indian?" Escalante said.

Nathan thought of Serafina. He should have let go of her weeks ago, but then, he wouldn't have had her that morning. *She wants to be mine.*

"She's a quite a thing. Raw, wild, like the desert."

Escalante went on.

"When you get tired of her, send her this way."

Nathan stood up.

"Are you gonna pay me or not?"

Escalante reached into his pocket and pulled out a large gold nugget.

"That's for the first mine I found for you. Let's have one for the other," said Nathan.

Escalante scoffed as he tossed another gold piece on the table. Nathan was an outsider to him, a tenderfoot at that. Escalante knew he was the sorcerer here. He would have Nathan's rancho and his woman, all in good time. He pulled out another nugget.

"I think you'll need this one too," he said, knowing from Della that Nathan would be short.

"What makes you think I need more?"

Escalante handed him a copy of the contract. Nathan twisted in his seat. An addendum had been added, trebling the tax.

"Just sign here," said Simon.

Nathan Goodwin was forced to sign over his soon to be acquired land, in the event of his demise, prior to the note being paid off.

"In the 1870's a man from the East Coast leased a sheep ranch, a few miles south of the pueblo, where he employed a young sheepherder. Infatuated with the man's lover, the shepherd began a surreptitious romance with her and followed her to the pueblo to plot against the easterner. A struggle ensued in the Elysian Grove amongst the three of them. The man managed to plunge his knife into the boy, grab the woman, and flee. The body of the youngster was unceremoniously buried where he fell - in a shallow grave, with no church rites. The women of the neighborhood appear at night for prayer. They believe that in forgiving the sinner, their own personal wishes will come true."
(Ida Flood Dodge, Old Pueblo Daily Star, 1919)

The golden glow of a sunset lit the lingering clouds from the passing storm and filtered through the glass into the room. Serafina again read the letter to Nathan from his fiancée, Clarissa Abbott. It had also been fixed to the back of one of the retablos. *Pesado!* I have meant nothing to him. So that was it. He was even less a man than she had imagined before. She settled into her metal tub of water, hot from the jar on the fire. She felt her mother damning her, for her sensuous nature, for her sins, real and imagined. She could still feel the strong hard grasp of the shepherd's hands as he groped her buttocks and pounded his life force into her. She ached for release from the voices inside that tormented her, drove her to disregard her sensibilities. The warm water soothed her soreness. Darkness came over the room. She lit a candle on the small ironwood table next to the tub. She fixed her sight on the blue glow.

Nathan pulled his soaked slicker off. The rain had cleared the sky of dust and the sun fell behind the lines of Black Mountain in a blaze of orange and red. He had dinner at Carlos' shack on the outskirts of Tucson. Albondigas, carne asada, fresh chiles, tortillas, fruit and flan. He left his horse at Rojo's livery and walked across the muddy, rutted street to the Occidental Hotel. He crossed through the noisy saloon and stood by the door leading out to the patio. The dimly lit yard showed up before him. A swirl of sound and sight presented itself: dancing boots, cowboy hats, cavalry hats, Mexican hats; bandanas dangling from rear pockets or festooned about hairy throats; cartridge belts and six-shooters; spurs, chaps; dancing calicoes, rebosas and lace mantillas; languorous and staccato and shrill voices; tipsy uncertain steps; a wheezing accordion, a driving harmonica and the sure notes of a violin played by Tito, the stable boy. He heard unintelligible oaths and proclamations. He smelled cheap perfume.

Perhaps this pandemonium could prove a panacea for the tumult he felt in his veins - for the fear of the knowledge of his lode being found out before the sale - for the unwelcome pain in his stomach when he thought of Serafina - and of Clarissa's impending arrival. He heard his grandfather's voice, "The eye in your belly knows the way."

"Howdy, stranger," said a voice at his side.

Nathan looked at the old man, whose eyes hid behind thin film.

"Name's Curran. What you see is the great cavalcade, all these different kinds moving through the west. It is their great adventure into the unknown world. Some will go farther, to the sea. Some will remain here. They are being swept on by the frontier, like tumbleweed, and some of them will likewise leave their seed behind. But remember, that seed must be enduring, the very best of its type, if it is to root itself in the soil."

Nathan rolled his eyes.

Curran winked, "Come on, let's have some fun."

The poker game was in full progress. Pull up a chair. Have a cigar. Some more whiskey. Deep into the night. Seven card high-low-roll-em. *Clarissa* - he rolled a red queen on the green felt table...*her soft long auburn hair, her clear green eyes, her blue blood.* He swirled another single malt shot back in his throat. *Serafina* - *why do you haunt me* - he rolled a black queen out. He placed the last nugget in the pot, behind his full house. The old man flipped his last card to reveal the four aces.

In a drunken wander of fear, amidst foul whispers, Nathan staggered up the stairs to his room, head in his hands.

"The spot commemorates the occasion when a gambler, who had lost his life savings, lured the man who had beat him to the grove. He shot and killed him where the wishing shrine is now located, near el ojito. Here, within a semi-circle of an adobe wall, blackened by thousands of candles, spotted with melted wax and ragged wreaths of artificial flowers, lies the altar upon his grave. Miracles are said to occur as a result of supplications made here."
(*Pepe Ochoa, Old Pueblo Daily Star, 1933*)

The house disappeared into the foothills as Serafina put the switch to the horse driving the small wagon. She stopped at the halfway station, tied up outside Café Carmelita, next to a large, teamster wagon.

Inside was a small room with dirt floors, three weathered wooden tables covered with frayed, hand-woven cloths. A bottle of picante stood in the center of each table next to a candle. Holy pictures were hung up around the room. The gaunt face of St. Francis peered down at her. The statue was hung from a rotting pine beam that separated the café from the kitchen.

Carmelita came in through the tattered sheet that served as the back door. She was dressed in black and humming softly. When the wrinkled brown lady saw Serafina, she smiled from her black eyes and grasped her hands.

"Ai," whispered the old one, "I see how you suffer."

Serafina went limp. Carmelita held her amiga to her bosom.

Birds flapped in takeoff from the tin roof.

"You must stay here," said the bruja, "The storm told me so."

Serafina collapsed into a chair. Carmelita went for coffee and pan.The teamster sat in a corner. He was rested. He had dropped part of his load at the mine and had spent the night there. The steaks, the whiskey and the talk with Escalante settled him. He had never felt better. He said nothing. All he could see was Serafina.

"I remember thinking, what are they fighting about - the young man, the beautiful girl and the tall, older man. They were loud, but no one was paying attention - there was a fiesta - the emigrants encamped around the grove had set up booths and games - many teamsters were there, enjoying themselves before continuing their journeys. It was blustery. I heard the girl mention the word gold - and the older man pushing the younger one. There was a knife. Then I was distracted. When I turned back, they were gone. It was later that the body was found." (Jose Martinez, on-looker, to George Hand, reporter for the Territorial, investigating the rumor of foul play at the grove, 1871)

Nathan was late. Della shifted the papers on her desk. She had followed Escalante's instructions. As much as she enjoyed the charm of the Boston man, she harbored resentments towards his eastern ways and his gift with the stick. Yet, she yearned for him - but Escalante was right, it was time to "turn him out."

"Just why the candles are lighted is not known to but few and none of these are very talkative, but there is a general belief among many of the superstitious that miracles have been wrought on this spot. The modus operandi is to place lighted candles about, murmur a prayer and leave it to burn through the night. The next morning the seeker returns. If the candle has been consumed or is still burning, the prayer will be answered. If it has blown out, it means hard luck. This place is called El Tiradito, which means castaway, discarded or abandoned, among other things. There are many old yarns about what happened here. What is certain is that prayerful propositions are made here to a nameless soul." (Old Pueblo Daily Star, 1951)

Serafina slipped through the curtain, following the melodious whistle of the shepherd.

"What are you doing here?" she said.

"There is a stink about. Your parents came by looking to take you with them back to Sonora. They were quite shaken that you were not there," said Juan.

"Take me to the spring," she said, "I must let him know about his child, so he has a chance to stand like a man."

"I saw a woman in a beautiful dress. She seemed quite disturbed, almost lost. A gringa, I've seen her before, went up to her. At that moment I felt my hair rise - heard a roar, and immediately a shaft of lightning struck across the pond in the trees. Someone said that someone died." (Cielo Avitia, on-looker, to George Hand, the Territorial, 1871)

"You clean up well, Nathan," said Della as he came through her door.

"Does everyone know everyone's business here," he said.

"I hear you have no business with me anymore," she said.

"On the contrary, although I have no direct payment for you, I have something more extraordinary." Nathan played his hole card. He told her about the gold lode on the property and offered to share all profits with her.

"Nathan, if what you say is true, I will be your partner, but you must do as I say, for this is very risky for us. Meet me at the grove at noon. Be ready to ride soon after."

"Nothing strange happened that day. There was a fiesta - some music, some drunks, some trade. Estorbo? No, I saw no foul play." (Pablo Murietta, teamster, on-looker, to George Hand, the Territorial, 1871)

The hawk flew high over Black Spring, spiraled above the cottonwood, desert willow, tamarisk, palo verde, ironwood and mesquite. The red bird caught Nathan's gaze while he walked his horse along the bank of the Rio Nuevo toward the grove, past the verdant fields of chilies, beans and maize. He heard the foreign chatter and spin of a group of Chinese emigrants, gathered around a small fire that held a spit of roasting duck. He cut up through the marsh, scattering gray mallards as he went, spores flying from reeds whistling in the wind. Up the hill to the spring, he whirled into the Elysian Grove, spun in an inner dance of flux and fear. His lungs heaved. He dismounted and leaned in rest against the trunk of a giant cottonwood, taking in the scene: many wagons parked askew under the trees around the water; tents and lean-to's scattered about the wild grass; hundreds of swarthy people mingled and lazed about. There was chatter, yell, bellow, smoke and rank smell. A group of Indians had donned wooden masks: dog, bird, frog, tiger and snake. He almost smiled as they danced. *I must find her.*

On the far side, he saw the stagecoach, propped up, wheel off.

He made his way along the water's edge, leaving the roan. *It must have broken down out here.* A small boy darted past, hurtling into the pond. He could make out Clarissa, in a long yellow dress, wearing her elongated hat. *What - no - I can't see her - no.*

Juan Oliveras palmed Nathan's shoulder, twisting him around to face Serafina.

"This is for you," she said, handing him the map and letter.

"Serafina," he said, "You're here...I..."

"I have one more thing for you," she lifted her blouse, exposing her stomach, breathing into it, pushing out the muscle walls.

He backed up, mouth agape. He instinctively slipped the rod from his sack, as if to make magic. He wheeled and stumbled toward the willow strand. *I am with your child...Nathan...please don't go.* He weaved through the trees. He looked back and saw her arms extended. He saw a man - *Simon* - approaching quickly up behind Serafina and Juan. He looked sidewise, towards Clarissa, who was in conversation with *Della. This is not the plan - this was never the plan - Serafina,* he whispered, "Serafina."

Nathan grabbed his gut and waved the wand as if to erase what he had seen. There seemed to be a scatter of movement. A great noise broke the air. A mysterious hand stretched in a shiver through the lace of a willow.

The Elysian Grove pulsed, dappled in the waning light of sun set through churning lavender clouds. The red hawk circled, flew off toward Black Mountain and was gone. Two teamsters dragged a body behind a tree for a quick, practiced burial. When they were done, they smoothed the area over with scuffed boots.

In the evening an emigrant couple laid their bright striped blanket on the soft dirt and slept in the starlight.

Serena

"**W**ho you callin fool?"
Riko rubbed his front tooth and swollen gums, but didn't say a word, just looked through her. She heard the baby cry and bolted, spilling her soda in his lap. He rocked up swinging wildly at her backside as she went into the bedroom. Serena gently scooped up the infant, turning to face Riko lurching into the room.

"Stay away from me freak," she said, her voice cracking.

He raised his hand.

"No, the baby!" She recoiled.

He lowered the clenched fist into the pointed finger.

"You bitch hoe!" He screamed.

"Dontchever call me a fool again!"

Serena looked into his glassy eyes and recognized nothing. No one home there, she thought, breaking into a belly-laugh, freeing up inside, rocking the baby tight to her chest.

Riko swung broadly into nothing but air, turning dizzily, careening out the door.

She heard the front door slam and knew that he was off to see the man, to see the sunrise on the dealer's porch, tootin his toots, drinkin that beer, retrieving dead butts from the garbage sack, too paranoid to go buy any more.

She got on the bus, Lisa in her back pack, totin her suitcase and headin for Carla's, again. Only this would be the last time. The last time. She closed her eyes as the bus lurched forward. She sang her lullabye, goodnight little Lisa goodnight.

Carla wasn't home and the key wasn't under the tired lookin rock in the garden.

"Ain't that the shits." She left the suitcase under the ramada and headed up the street to the corner store, where all the young gafflin wannabe's hung out. There was a line for the phone.

"Hey, Serena!"

She looked over and eyed Leo. What in the name was he doing there.

He came over, all 55 years of him, in his fancy suit, with that wide open look of his and he bent down and kissed the top of the baby's head.

"Sup Leo?"

Leo laughed. He loved the way she talked, so soft with her unimaginable lingo. She had worked as a janitor at his law firm for the past six months and he always enjoyed listening to her stories. The sheer hell and desperation of her life didn't jive with her spirit, not one bit. It was as if the insane events were merely grist for a genuine inner knowing which always came out in this incredible smile, in this redeeming authentic embracing laugh. He knew that she knew what was going on in this life and that he didn't have a clue. He wanted her more than anything that life had presented him. More than the big bucks, more than the smarts, more than wonderful family, more than the good life. Not one person in his whole life had ever known. Serena did, and that was enough. Damn the 35 year age difference, damn it all.

"Nothing. I was just stopping to pick up some smokes."

"Shount smoke Leo," she giggled.

"Hell," he laughed, "you told me you smoked until you got pregnant."

"So!"

She loved to tease him. He had been very understanding of her situation and often allowed her to work extra hours. He just seemed to enjoy her company and made no demands on her, giving her a rest from Riko and the endless fights. Oh, she loved Riko alright. He was the father of her child and a fine lookin guy when she first met him. Dope time had made him look like the ugly stick done got him good. He was real crazy now, real crazy. She smiled at the thought of him, the real him and wished with all her might that he was still there, that he was still home.

Leo sensed a twinkle in her eyes that he had never seen before. "Can I give you a lift?"

"You mean, ride, Leo?"

Riko came out of his dark reverie in time to stop the drool from rolling down his chin on to his jacket. He swung his head slowly back and forth, rolling it round and round, trying intuitively to undo the freeze in his spine. He wheeled down Potter Street, trying to wake up, to sift things out. He knew that he had been in another fight with Serena, that he had gone to Chubb's, loaded up, gone home and she was gone. He passed out a while and now here he was lookin for her. Christ, he couldn't take it anymore! His head was banging up against itself, roaring inside. All his head said was that he loved her and the baby and would do anything at all for that. He drove on, weaving towards Carla's.

Riko recognized Leo's BMW pulling out of the corner store. He saw Serena in the shotgun seat as they passed by going the other way. He hit the breaks hard and made a quick u-turn.

He rammed Leo's car hard from the rear, almost tearing his bumper off. Leo punched the accelerator.

At the intersection of 22nd and Darton, Riko managed to get alongside them. He looked blankly in at Serena and saw once again that she knew what he would never know. He saw his child and a tear formed in his eye. He thought he heard Serena's deep laugh. He yanked the wheel sharply, ramming the nose of his Chevy into the side of the BMW, rolling it over and flipping the Chevy end over end, leaving both cars overturned, their wheels spinning in the black sky.

The paramedic cradled the infant. She was so beautiful, the only survivor. He thought that she looked like she knew something that he would never know.

First Song

When the scholarship to Notre Dame failed to materialize, I headed down to the Great Desert University, on a full ride. I should have joined the Jesuits.

The head coach, K. Kenny King, welcomed us in the glaring August sun of 1963. He called us his "Green Futures" and told us to be ready to run the opening opponents plays against his varsity squad in three days.

Our freshman coach, a seventh year graduate student named Looper, taught us to "stride," to run with our thumbs and forefingers stuck together. I thought it silly, but after going up against the varsity for the first time, realized it was a meditative device, that by concentrating on your fingers you didn't have time to worry about your immanent impalement by a 240 pound linebacker.

The pattern of mayhem was established early on. The varsity was big and bad, but they rarely scored! The coaches, fearing for their jobs, took it out on the varsity who took it out on us peach fuzzed frosh.

"Just another battle," Boonie would giggle, as half a dozen of us sat around each afternoon on the chipped linoleum of my dorm room at Bamm Hall, listening to the radio, awaiting practice.

"Don't care if I do die!" Rhino screamed.

Everyone screamed back, "As long as it's on the football field!"

Then the 3:30 news would come on and we'd get religiously quiet, knowing that we'd soon be in pads under the fat yellow sun. After the news, Piggy would yell, "Great Balls of Fire!" We'd all get up, butt shoulders, yell, dance and jump to the first song after the news.

We'd crowd out the door with the collective dirge of "Don't care if we do die, do die, do!"

I was a quarterback, but we were all just a bunch of ineligible green jerseys to the coaches, finding ourselves playing any position. During the confusion of one practice, when the green shirts were split up into two or three groups to be punished by the big bad varsity, Boonie and I developed a code to track each other and our sanity. In the midst of being blocked, tackled or otherwise bullied, we'd spontaneously yell "Cracker!" The coaches were unable to stop it, and the "Cracker" call spread throughout the green shirts, like a Spartacus rallying cry.

Coach King would often be forced to discipline us, though, for our general lack of respect for those with authority or eligibility. He'd pick one of us at random who would have to tackle every single green shirt, one at a time, until a trainer was summoned to administer a "popper," a giant salt tablet that was shoved down his parched gullet.

We were known as the "Pups," in deference to the varsity's "Bulldogs." The Pups only played a couple of games against other freshmen teams, and they were ragged affairs, nowhere near as glorious as our long lost high school games had been. Clipped from grace, we got our revenge, late on Monday afternoons, at the Toilet Bowl. We would scrimmage those members of the varsity who hadn't played or who had played poorly in losing the previous Saturday varsity game. They just couldn't score. The Toilet Bowl was played without benefit of officials, sideline markers or goal lines. The only hold barred was Katie, as in "Katie bar the door." The game ended in sweat, blood and grime in the gathering darkness. Cries of "Cracker" swept towards the locker room.

At nights we relaxed in the swamp-cooled splendor of Bamm Hall. We played Lackawanna Ball (hallway handball) or Ceiling Ball (roughhouse ping-pong, played by bouncing a tennis ball off the ceiling on to a coffee table, with a towel for a net). The air was filled with the aromatic fragrance of sweaty jocks and noxema. Ace Dewald, a six-foot two, 277 pound insomniac, the meanest lineman the varsity had, would set off the fire alarms on our floor every morning at 3 a.m. Thanks, Ace!

The Bulldogs continued to lose. Coach King lost his voice, his poise, and, with his job on the line, freshmen ballplayers began disappearing. We had started with 85 guys, 25 on scholarship and the rest "walk-ons." By November, there were only 30 of us left and that number was dwindling. Boonie joined the Marines with convulsive laughter. Rhino was suspended for identifying rocks as minerals, flunking his geology mid-term. Fuzzy, a six foot six, 190 pounder, was only allowed one helping per meal. Starving, he went home to Alabama where he became a consensus All-American and later, a pro-bowler with the Bears. Ollie fractured his pelvis in a car crash one night after attempting to drive from the Lazy Horse Bar back to the dorm, backwards. Matu left after breaking an assistant coach's nose who had grabbed Matu's face mask and shook his head while making insulting comments about his family's origin, one to many times. Big Joe Butcher walked away from it all the day after Kennedy was assassinated. Joe refused to practice on a national day of mourning. "It's gone too far," he said.

I stayed on until the last week. There were twelve freshmen left. On Monday, Bassey and I were forced to return punts against the varsity for 45 minutes. Two against eleven. On one kick, I caught the first would be tackler with a flying foot in the groin and Bassey somehow broke through the onslaught of tacklers for a touchdown. We didn't know whether to laugh or cry, knowing that they couldn't score.

On Tuesday, I decided that I just couldn't reschedule my geology field trip. On Wednesday I turned up sick at the university infirmary. I put my fingers down my throat after every meal and stayed until Sunday. The varsity lost their final game, to their arch-rival Mill U., 23 to 0.

The next week Coach King dropped by to tell me that my scholarship was in jeopardy and that I'd have to run 25 "stadiums" for missing all those practices. I ran the stadiums under the coach's unsmiling, hooded eyes and was one of 8 freshmen to play Spring ball. The coach vowed "renewed punch" for the fall, but he lost me. I did join the Jesuits. I only lasted six months. The priests thought I had psychological problems. They could forgive me for always going around with my thumbs and forefingers glued together, but they couldn't stomach my piercing screams whenever I heard music: "Don't care if I do die!"

Dog Days Night

Duke flushed as he scanned the program. He nudged his faded buddy in the ribs.

"What!" said Blackie.

"Narrow Line."

"Nah, no way, Dukey."

"It's a lock, chocolate man, a dead solid lock."

"She's a maiden, you idiot, runnin against The Dog, my dog, Turbo Tina, queen of the A Class!"

"Look, jerkie, we're takin it all downtown on Narrow Line, the 5 dog. Look at that speed, we can break it!"

Blackie knew that he was stuck again with the big man's plan. What a fuckin dumb oaf. If he hadn't been so tanked he would have taken him on, called him out, slapped some sense into him.

"Ah, okay, Duke."

"Good boy, Black, you won't regret it," said Duke. He jabbed him in the ribs again, "You won't forget it, either. Just pony up that big wad of yours, Black."

Blackie peeled ten one hundred dollar bills from his pocket, the rent for his apartment, all he had and he hated himself for telling Duke about it.

Duke headed toward the windows. Blackie thought he looked like a giant boogie man hoofing his way across the black scuff of linoleum littered with crumpled dead dream tickets. He gulped, grimaced and spit - sure as hell all his money was about to be gone.

The dog boxes were set on the far side of the track, a long race, one and half times around.

Blackie felt the bell ring in his groin. Duke stood with him, leaning over the trackside fence, shielding his eyes from the rain. Duke had Narrow Line covered every which way – Quinella, Trifecta Wheel and On The Nose.

Duke's high-pitched scream pierced Blackie's heart as the eight dogs broke around the first turn. Narrow Line, wearing red No. 5, was THIRTY yards ahead as they streaked in front of the boys the first time past the long finish line mirrors. "See, Black, See!" said Duke, banging him in the ribs one more time, "Go baby!" Narrow Line opened up a HUNDRED yard lead around the backstretch and turned into the final loop.

Blackie saw it – he saw Narrow Line give way. Her front paws buried in the muck in the last turn, flipped her face down in the mud, sent her end over end into the fence.

Duke turned to ash as the other seven dogs flashed across the finish. His mouth opened wide, soundless. He turned towards Blackie. Duke was too late to see the haymaker. The punch came his way, from down low, from way down inside Blackie's soul, from the hot center of the earth itself and slammed up into his nose, twisting his hulking frame over the rail, head down in the mud.

Narrow Line limped towards the finish, down the fence line. She halted at Duke's sprawling body and licked his bloody nose.

Blackie clanged through the swinging doors of the front exit with a scream, "Here comes the rabbit, rabbit, rabbit!"

The Cracked House

I n the backyard garden of a small hotel, white-laced curtains blew with the chill morning breeze through the open windows of a small guest cottage. Davey packed his knapsack while his recorder played *Daniel and the Sacred Harp* by the Band. He stuffed in his extra pair of levis, an embroidered Mexican shirt, a Brazilian butterfly stash box, a small painted ceramic frog, a copy of *Nadja* by Andre Breton, a soiled sketch book, charcoals and pastels wrapped in cellophane. He stood, cued his recorder to Steppenwolf's *America*, threw his Dodger baseball cap on, flung the pack over his shoulder and strolled across the garden.

He found a tram to Amsterdam's Central Station and wandered inside the train cathedral for a cup of coffee. He headed down Damrak Street in the hustle and blur, strolled on the cobblestone amidst a flurry of pigeons in Damsquare. Across the dam, hundreds of young people hugged the steps to the national war monument, talking, sleeping, playing music. The smell of hash hung in the air. He darted through the tie-dyed crowd and went back up Damrak to the American Express office, where many young people were gathered, visiting, buying and selling, exchanging information. Davey noticed a long-haired freak with a fringe jacket, sitting on an old Harley Davidson motorcycle. The bike was for sale.

"Hey man, what's going on," said Davey. "Nice bike, how much you want for it?"

"2100 guilders," said the freak.

"Too much for me. Say, like to buy some weed? I got a couple lids, and, uh, I need some money. Just skipped out on the army, gotta put something together, you know. It's good weed, good old Mexican mota. Look man, I'm for real. I used to have the long hair. Name's Davey." He extended his hand.

The freak stared at him and shook it.

"I'm Billy, Motorcycle Billy. I'm selling out too. Business ain't been so good. Case of the continuing war, I call it. Hop on, Davey!" He flung himself on to the back of the bike, clutching his pack and his recorder. Off they flew, back past the Dam and out of sight towards Nieuwmarkt.

Billy sputtered down the Zeedijk, running along a canal, turning into a narrow alley leading to Geldersekade, stopping in front of a dilapidated gabled house, four stories high, #44. Billy chained the bike to a lamp post.

"Got to do this," said Billy. "There are these outrageous characters here. The provos. They believe that essential things should be free. Houses, bikes, cars. Some of them live right here. This is my pad. It's a cracked house. Condemned in this case, but free if you move in, crack it. There's a housing shortage here. Lots of young Dutch and foreigners live in places like this. I live here with some friends from the states, but this place is getting kinda hot. It's right in line with the new metro subway. See that concrete slab over there. Well, it's coming this way and we'll all be pushed out. Guess they want to move the people out to the boonies so they can ride the subway back to where they started out to begin with. The cops keep trying to get us to leave, but the Dutch people inside are resisting them. Won't be long though. Come on in, I could use some smoke. Don't see much weed around here, mostly hash."

Davey followed the sound of Billy's steps up the steep dark stairwell. He passed some open doors and saw empty rooms, bare with holes. Rats scurried in the pale light coming through tall windows. The stairs ended abruptly at a ceiling. Billy knocked with two hard raps and two soft. There was the sound of metal on wood and a hatch opened above them. They went into the ceiling, into the roost.

Davey met Billy's friends, Lia and Thomas. Lia heated him some tea on the kerosene burning pipe stove which stood by a low table separating the kitchen, with its rotting cupboards, from a long living area. The end of the room had two, eight-foot windows, that shed the same curious golden light that once lit Vermeer's eyes. Both long walls were painted in free form with various sketches, pictures and graffito. A faded blue couch ran along one wall and above, a cardboard sculpture that resembled the number 9. Davey walked towards the windows. The red of dusk overtook the golden glow. He could see an old church steeple with a golden rooster on top. He heard seven bells ring and looked below the clock on the spire and saw a year in relief in gold leaf, 1614. His gaze pierced the gathering night, skimming the rooftops of another world.

"Davey, you okay. Come here, I'll show you the back view, then we can get down to some Afghani smoke." Billy ushered him down a back hall into a back room, and slid open an old warehouse door which revealed a u-shaped courtyard and the rest of the condemned building, all in great disrepair. Davey froze, then trembled at the height, the floating vacancy, the building skeleton and the gathering night. Billy saw this and slammed the door shut.

Davey sank into the couch. Thomas handed him an ivory chillum wrapped in a bright scarf, filled with hash. He showed him how to hold it, lit the pipe and watched the glaze come to Davey's eyes. There was a knock on the trap door and Lia pulled up on the latch to let in two men and a woman. An older man, Koos, handed her some fresh flowers and kissed her on the cheek. Billy and Thomas greeted Koos, Marion and Jan with embraces and introduced them to Davey, who managed a meager murmur and half glance.

"Where did he come from? Better watch out Billy, he might be police," said Jan. Lia turned on her recorder and played Dylan's *It's Alright Ma, I'm Only Bleeding*.

"Another war casualty," said Billy. "He wanted to sell me some marijuana, crazy, huh. He's for real though, just look at him." Billy sat eyes closed deep in the couch.

"Goddamn, what do *they* want from us?" Said Marion. "He looks like I feel. I'm so sad about this sickness, this sickness is everywhere."

"Ja. Ja. Het zietke, it' everywhere. It will go though, go away, we will see it go, too."

"Stop it. Have some of this stuff," said Thomas. "Good for the sickness."

"If it doesn't make you sicker," said Lia.

Marion smiled her infectious smile, her upper lip wrapped up towards her nose, and broke into a deep laugh. "Ja, the cure, better to talk about the cure. Holland is sinking everyday into the sand. I have my cure, my boat. I will sail away to my uncle's schuilplaats in the Lofoten Islands, hide away from the sickness and the shrinking earth. Hide anywhere I can. This place, it's a hiding place, too, all hide away. It's like children's tag, the hiding place and then, home free!"

"Ja, ja," said Jan. "Home free. Look how low your friend goes, Billy, passed out. Maybe he would want to stay on my boat with my family. It would be safer for him."

"Sounds good, Jan," said Billy. "Marion, could Davey stay in that room next to yours, until he can go to Jan's, it's pretty crowded up here."

"He is welcome, if he wants," she said.

The group sat around in a loose circle, with Davey asleep in the middle. They talked about the war, mixing Dutch with English, sipping on Grolsch beer and soup, munching on old cheese and fresh bread, rolling their own cigarettes with black tabak. Jan picked up Billy's old Guild guitar and began to strum. Davey stirred and could hear Jan's deep baritone sing Leadbelly's *Goodnight Irene*.

The room had peeled paint and was barren except for a sleeping bag spread out in a corner next to two large windows that looked out into the dingy grey courtyard. Davey lay curled on the bag. His tape recorder played *Sweet Child* by Pentangle. He wandered in his mind, playing out his trip from Fort Belvoir, Virginia to Amsterdam, a long strange trip indeed. He closed his eyes and fell into a dream, a pixilation of images fell through his cells: an army doctor, seated behind a desk, says, "If I gotta do it, you gotta do it;" a deserted country road twisting through a sea of hills in a gathering fog; a Vietnam firefight in rice paddy muck; a coach screaming at him saying, "You got too many irons in the fire;" Johnny Unitas firing a sideline pass to Raymond Berry; the Big Sur coastline, looking south from Nepenthe; a body surfer catching the curl of a wave; Meher Baba, smiling; a belly dancer whirling in a crowded restaurant; cluster bombs along a jungle coastline; a coyote pack in the desert...a pounding, a pounding on the door. Davey sat up, startled. Marion appeared.

"What is it, are you all right?" She said.

"No more. I just want to sleep," he said.

"I brought you some lunch."

"No, I'm not hungry." He looked away.

"You must eat. Then you should get up and go for a walk, perhaps you could find some work. You must do something. You can't just lay there all day, it won't just happen for you."

"Go away," he said.

Marion put down the food she had brought. She turned to him at the door, "Nobody really cares about anybody else, you know." She slammed the door. The tape whirred, at its end. Davey leaned over and put in *Where Do the Children Play* by Cat Stevens. He pulled off the butt end of the fresh loaf of bread.

Jan, his huge frame wrapped in a grey Russian army coat and a yellow neck scarf, and Davey, bundled by his olive drab field coat, sat outdoors at the Café Rokit on the *Rembrandtsplein*. They drank pils, rolled cigarettes, and took it all in. The drama on the square unfolded before them: costumed street performers; an old organ grinder replete with monkey; business men and women on the move; refugees from far-flung countries; hippies of all stripes; shoppers and cinema goers, most wearing Dutch clogs, even the cops.

"Ja, you look well, Davey," said Jan. He raised his glass. "Heildronk! A salute to you and your Amsterdam adventure!" They tapped their beers together.

"Thanks, Jan. I feel much better now, stronger. It's funny how you go. I guess I'm going to make it," said Davey, touching his heart, "in here, and out there, wherever the hell I am and with whoever the hell you crazy people are!"

"Ja, ja. I am you and you are me and we are both midwives delivering gardens of Eden to each other and all we meet!"

"Man, you are batshit! Say, is it cool for me to stay here, or what?"

"Maybe," said Jan. "You could seek legal harbor here, there is an unofficial sanction for this. You could live underground and do black jobs. You could move to Sweden and get official sanction or you could hide out almost anywhere in Europe. You could also go back, Davey, before it's too late. Give yourself a little time to decide, come stay on the boat with us for a while, then you will see what is to happen for you."

Everything is so old, thought Davey as he entered the foyer of the seventeenth century warehouse in the Jordaan district. Four guys and two girls mingled outside an interior doorway. A guy and a girl read to each other from sheets of paper. Jan blustered in, slapped Davey on the back, recognized one of the guys.

"Teo, this is Davey, the one I was telling you about. You think he could try out for the movie. He could use some work."

"Ja. We will all be stars! This is the last day of the audition," said Teo. He hands Davey a script. "Read this, then, when we call you in, you will read for us and towards the middle of the reading, you will take your clothes off as you read, okay."

"Huh, a porno!" Said Davey.

"Ja, life is profane! You said you wanted work," said Jan.

"To tell the truth, Davey, you don't have much chance to get a big part. If you had a girl with you it would be better, couples work out easier," said Teo.

"I should bring Ankie down here for an audition."

"Right, Jan, your wife would love it. Maybe I should ask Marion," said Davey.

In a corner of the warehouse studio, Jan stands over Teo and two young women who are running the audition. They are seated behind a small table with a monitor on it. There is a video camera set up in front of them, directed at a small bare stage area, lit by one large standing floodlight. Davey was summoned.

"Go ahead, Davey, stand on that mark over there," said Teo.

"Should I start," said Davey. "Okay, here goes. *The Love Song of J. Alfred Prufrock* by T.S. Eliot." Davey started awkwardly, like a sheep getting up from the shears. *"Let us go then, you and I, When the evening is spread out against the sky Like a patient etherized upon a table; Let us go, through half-deserted streets, The muttering retreats Of restless nights in cheap hotels And sawdust restaurants with oystershells: Streets that follow like a tedious argument of insidious intent To lead you to an overwhelming question."* Davey kicks off his shoes. *"Oh, do not ask, What is it? Let us go and make our visit."* He removes his shirt and his voice quickened. *"The yellow fog that rubs its back upon the window panes."* He removed his pants and his voice broke. *"Licked its tongue into the corner of the evening."* He took off his boxer shorts and stood naked except for his black socks. *"Lingered upon the pools that stand in drains."* Jan choked back laughter in the background. *"Let fall upon its back the soot that falls from chimneys, Slipped by the terrace, made a sudden leap, And seeing that it was a soft October night, curried once about the house, and fell asleep."*

Jan broke and scurried out of the room. Davey squinted and shrugged his shoulders.

"Goed Davey, bedank," said Teo.

He continued to read in mock disgust. *"And indeed there will be time,"* he crumpled the pages and bent over to retrieve his shorts.

The ramshackle booths of the flea market spread haphazardly across the Niewmarkt square. Davey strolled along and was drawn to a table by the penetrating gaze of an old gypsy woman who was selling hand woven medallions, pagan scapulars, diamond and circular in shape, embroidered with stars, half-moons, waves, hearts and smiles. He examined the cloth necklaces. He pulled his tape recorder from his pack.

"Is it all right for me to try and sell this here?" He said.

"Eistelu, compa!"

"What?"

"Eistelu, compa!" She gestured for him to do as he pleased. He set out the recorder and put in Paul Horn's *Inside*. The gypsy rocked her shoulders gently, turned and smiled. Davey barked at a tattered hipster sauntering in front of the booth.

"Hey, like to buy a recorder and tapes."

"How much"

"Fifty bucks, including all the tapes."

"Wow, must be hot."

"Nah, I just need the money."

"Eistelu, compa," said the gypsy.

"What's she talking about," said the hippie.

"I don't know," said Davey.

"Well, give me some time, I gotta round up some geetus."

The gypsy twinkled and hummed and pulled some bills from a coin purse and handed them to him.

51

"Eistelu, compa."

"You want it," he said

"Eistelu, compa."

"It's a deal. I sure hate to lose those tapes." He pushed the recorder and tapes over to her. She handed him one of her medallions as he turned to leave.

"Thanks, enjoy the music," he said.

"Eistelu, compa."

He walked briskly down the aisle, rounding another booth and smacked head on into Marion. They gasped and let out a roar when they recognized that they had run into each other.

"Hi, I sold it, for fifty dollars," he said.

"Goed," she said, "Should get you through until you find work."

"What the hell, let's go celebrate," he said.

"Davey, that's for food."

"So, let's go eat."

He placed the medallion over her head and swung his arm under hers and they made their way into the mix of the crowd.

They spent the next few days entwined. She showed him the sights, from the Reichsmuseum to the Van Gogh Museum, from Haarlem to Delft to the beaches of Scheveningen. He even learned how to say Scheveningen, in the choking, gutteral Dutch way. They shed their shoes and raced through the deserted dunes, rolling down the sand mounds to the sea. They splashed each other, drew designs in the wet sand, skipped rocks and mocked seagulls. They embraced as the orange sun got geometric, step-sided, as it set in the North Sea.

There was an hour to spare before he had to meet Jan for some labor work on a building on Prinsengracht. Davey crossed a canal bridge and meandered down a narrow alley to the White Owl Pub. It was packed with seamen, whores, hippies and businessmen. All became quiet when Davey entered, except for a few tinkling glasses, a pronounced lull. He paused in concern, stepped up to the bar and ordered a pils. As the bartender filled his glass, the place just as suddenly filled with noise and activity. He shook his head, found a small table against the poster filled wall, sat down and scanned the Herald Tribune. A rugged, strack young man approached.

"Howdy, mind if I join you," said the man.

"No, please yourself."

"Name's Jimmy Thompson."

"Davey Havens."

"Pleased to meet you. You American?"

"Yea," said Davey, "I'm from Tucson."

"Texas, myself, born in Dibol, raised in Nacadoches. Been here about a year now. Kissed the army off and came here."

"You a deserter?"

"Might put it that way, except, I got all that straightened out."

"How's that," said Davey

"Met this fella here. I did some work for him and he got me off the hook. Worked out real good. I still owe him, so I can't go back to the States yet, maybe in time."

"You in Nam?"

"A grunt for eight months, platoon sergeant in the Highlands, saw half of my men blown away, way away. Went on R and R and never looked back. Nasty, greedy war, got nothing to do with communism, no sir, it's all about what's in the Gulf of Tonkin, dope in the triangle, and power. No way to win, no way," said Jimmy.

"Yea, makes no sense, not one bit. They cut me orders to go over there, I cut my own orders to come over here," said Davey.

"I guess that makes us a bit related."

"I guess, so there's a way out of all this?"

"No, no way out."

"Look," said Davey standing, " I gotta go, but I'd like to meet this guy your talking about. I'm living now over on this boat with a Dutch family. Here's the address, over on the Nieuendammerdijk."

"No, I think it's best you go your way. We all gotta go our own way."

Davey found the group of Dutch workers working on the façade of a small, old hotel, squeezed between two larger converted warehouses on the wide canal street. Jan, his face covered in plaster, handed Davey a sledgehammer and sent him inside to smash down walls.

The Nieuendammerdijk laid out along a cut off of the Amstel River. It stretched for a mile or so and was lined with 13th century houses facing the water and the canal boats tied up to the dijk. Jan and David plodded across a wooden ramp to a boat, the Pax A'Dam, and disappeared into the pilot-house. After dinner with Jan, his wife Ankie and the baby Kiki, Davey thanked them and stepped up towards the deck.

"Sloep lekker," said Jan.

He walked along the length of the boat alongside the freight compartment, 90 feet to the stern, and disappeared down a hatch.

Below he sat at a small table in a tiny triangle shaped alcove cabin. A kerosene lamp burned and he sketched meticulously. A picture of Hopalong Cassidy was propped on his desk. His black work with the Dutch boys had given him a new recorder. He pushed the button. *Take Me to the Pilot* by Elton John accompanied his drawing strokes. He finished his warm Amstel Beer, rolled a final cigarette, flicked down the lamp wick and climbed into his sleeping bag in the oddly shaped bunk. He did not think and was not pursued by thoughts.

In the main shipping lane in the middle of the Amstel River, a huge freighter approached a small rowboat head on. Jan and Davey stroked furiously.

"Faster. Haasten," said Jan.

The rowboat rode the wake of the giant ship, just avoiding a collision. They abandoned their oars, clapped and laughed. Davey stood and raised both hands triumphantly, before losing his balance, rocking the boat and sending them both into the chill of the river.

Davey walked up Damrak, headed back to the dijk, carrying a full white laundry bag slung over his shoulder. He went past the American Express office, remembering his meeting with Billy, smiling at his fate, and came alongside the McDonald's. He glanced into the window and his eyes met the eyes of a young woman behind the glass. His sister, Mona stared at him in astonishment. After hugs, he joined her and her husband, Lou, inside.

"God, you're so skinny. I'll get you a couple of cheeseburgers," said Lou.

"Ja, ja," said Davey, "Looks like my brother-in-law has been eating his fair share of cheeseburgers. Thanks, Lou. So, how are you, Mona."

"This is unbelievable, finding you. We were just ready to go, Lou has to get back to the base at Sembach. We've been up here for three days looking for you. When the folks got your letter, they called and said that maybe we could find you. We tried everything. The police said that you were probably underground, they said something about "cracked" houses. Lou tried to get some information on the streets, but nobody was any help. What luck," she said.

"Yea, amazing. You're looking good. How's the baby?"

"She kicks a lot. Sometimes I think I can hear her."

It's a "he" Mona," said Lou. "Here Davey, eat your guts out, you look like a broomstick."

"Better a broomstick than a balloon. How's the Air Force. The war hasn't spread to Germany, yet, has it."

"I got nothing to do with the damn Vietnam War. I'm just a glorified telephone operator. I piped in the Super Bowl to the whole base and sold the feed on the side to some German television guy. If they find out, it's my ass."

"You could probably afford to lose that," said Davey.

"Davey, Dad says that if you turn yourself in soon, that Congressman Calihan will do what he can to help you get a discharge. If you wait, though, you might go to jail, or spend your life over here," said Mona.

"Hiding out. Home free."

"What."

"Nothing. Look, I've never felt better or stronger about what I believe in. I'm sick of living my life for the idiots who run this crazy world and try to cram their rotten concepts and orders down my throat."

"Bah, you're such an absolutist. We all have to put up with that crap, it's just the way it is," said Lou.

"It's not me," said Davey.

"Oh, Davey, you make me so mad," said Mona, "You think the whole world turns around you. There are lots of people who love you, you owe them something."

"Yea, I owe them. Me. The real me, not some gladboy, All-American."

"Goddam, it's not that simple," said Lou.

"Don't you think that you could do what you're talking about back home. Give yourself a chance, you could always come back here if you wanted," she said.

"I don't know, so much has happened, all kinds of people, feelings, the light here. It's funny how you go."

"I hate to say this, but you've lost touch with reality. You can't give the whole world the finger," said Lou.

"Lou's right. Go back and face it. Get out of this mess. Things will look different to you then."

"Things look different right now," said Davey, "I've got to follow my path, to where I'm not sure. Look, I appreciate your concern, your love. I'll let you know what I'm going to do. Somehow, I feel that everything is all right."

"I don't want to hear it," said Mona, "You're just talking a lot of words. Look around, at what's going on, where you are, where you're headed."

"What is going on. If you don't want to hear it, you won't. Go back to the base. I'll call you. Take care of the baby. Skip rope, Lou."

Lou handed Davey an airline ticket.

"The plane leaves for New York tomorrow at 6.p.m."

They were gathered on the deck of the Pax A'Dam. Jan, Ankie, Kiki, Davey, Marion, and a lawyer named Gerard. Food and pils were plentiful.

"What would my risk be, then, in seeking legal asylum," said Davey.

"The main one, of course," said Gerard, "would be deportation and court martial, especially since you would have publicly embarrassed your government. There is no official policy of the Dutch government to grant sanctuary to people in your position. One U.S. Naval officer did receive unofficial permission to stay. He was married to a Dutch girl, though. I would be willing to help you if you choose to pursue a legal course of action."

"Thanks, Gerard. I'm not sure I want to be a test case, though." Davey went over and sat down next to Marion, their legs dangled from the edge of the boat. They could see their reflections in the water below.

"You have the finest smile," said Davey as he kissed her forehead, "I haven't seen you for a few days, but I've been thinking about you."

"Goed. I've been moving my possessions to another house. They have already blocked off the street and are working day and night on the metro line."

"What will happen when the police come to remove you from the house?"

"We will protest, then to jail."

Everyone moved toward the bow to salute the sunset. Jan had Kiki in his arms, swaying back and forth.

"Heildronk! My friends, we all fly with Kiki," said Jan, moving the child like a bird, "above the sea, above the earth, and to the stars." Kiki shrieked like the seagulls plying for food around the ship.

Marion and Davey sat in her room in the cracked house later that night. Her frayed protest flag rested on a wooden stick in the corner. She had put on *Blue* by Joni Mitchell.

"You shouldn't stay here," she said.

"Don't you want me here?"

"No, it's too dangerous and I want to be alone."

"I'd like to stay awhile," he said.

"What do you want from me?"

"Nothing. I'm just wondering what the hell I'm going to do. You are the most important person in my life."

"That's crazy."

"Not to me, I, I love you very much. I, I want to be with you."

"I'm not in love with you or anyone else," she said. "I like you, but I can't give you what it seems you want."

"We could work things out, together, couldn't we?"

"Nay, I have nothing to give you now."

"What about the beautiful times we've had."

"There will be other times."

"I don't understand. I don't know what to do."

"If you don't know, nobody else does. Please go Davey."

Sympathy for the Devil blared from the huge speakers in the cavernous Milkweg Club. The former milk factory had itself been cracked and the Provos had later received a government subsidy to turn it into a youth free zone. The Rolling Stones themselves would have been proud. Davey weaved his way through the haze of whirling dancers, pulsing to a light show, to back rooms where hundreds of young people, dressed in a freakish array of attire are drinking, playing table games, and smoking hashish. He stepped over bodies lying up against the walls of the rooms and felt the old urge. The hash dealer pulled out his blocks and pieces of the dope.

"Hey, man, how do you get out of here," said Davey.

"What, you don't want to buy," said the dealer.

Davey grabbed him by the arm.

"Where can I get some smack?"

"Whoa, you gotta be kiddin, man. Sure you wanna do that? Okay, see the guy down by the Skinny Bridge."

Davey walked along in the soft night glitter of a canal street. He asked a woman for directions to the bridge. Keep on going. He came to the old bridge with the wooden frame, an old canal drawbridge. He started across, stopped, took out some shag and rolled a cigarette. An oriental man dressed in black crossed the bridge in front of him.

"Excuse me, is this the Skinny Bridge?"

"You say," said the man.

"The Skinny Bridge."

The man laughed, the deepest laugh that Davey had ever heard, and went on. Davey turned and stared down the canal, smoking. He heard strong breathing behind him and turned around. The oriental man was doing a slow dance in the center of the bridge. His face was lit up as he lifted his legs and flowed and bent and flew, then slid slowly off the bridge, as if on water, laughing again. He watched him go, rolled some more shag. From out of the blackness, he heard a voice.

"Dude, got some fine smack here, the works."

Jan played billiards with some friends at the pub in Nieuendammerdijk. Gerard careened in from the outside glare.

"Jan, the cracked house, politie everywhere."

He put down his cue and they ran to Gerard's two seat Citroen. When they arrived they saw hundreds of protestors, chanting and carrying signs denouncing the metro. Fifty or so police were there. A demolition crew and their equipment awaited the clearing of the house. Marion's flag hung from her window. The police shouted through their megaphones. *Come out.*

Davey dropped and stretched out face down in the grass in Vondelpark, next to the lake. He closed his eyes to children's squeals.

Davey was four, yet not taller than the average three year old, a freckled wisp of a child. He held tightly to the rope tied through a hole in the end of his broomstick and said "giddyap." His friend Ricky followed suit, shooting at him with his right index finger "bam, bang." They rode in a dull grey rain down a dirt street to the edge of the small farming town. A leafless tree stood along a strong flowing open irrigation ditch that crossed under the road through a small metal pipe. Davey ran ahead, but Ricky had scrambled quickly up the tree, shooting down at him "bam, bang." Davey turned, shooting back. He heard the crack and saw Ricky fall with the limb from the tree. The rushing water sucked him towards the pipe. When he got to the edge of the ditch all he saw were Ricky's legs disappearing into the dark hole. He ran to the other side, but Ricky didn't come out. Davey gasped and looked around. He ran, dragging his stick horse with him, ran back up the dirt road until he couldn't breathe, ran a mile to the crossroads, where Ricky's father ran the store. "Who is it?" said the man, hearing Davey's wheeze. He grabbed the blind man's hand and pulled him out the door. They ran together hand in hand.

"He's in the water, in the pipe!" The man lowered himself into the cold water and flailed his hands. Davey grabbed him and showed him the opening to the pipe. The man grabbed the edge and lowered himself feet first into the tunnel. He kicked, hunched, moaned and kicked again. He yelled for the boy to go to the other side and see if Ricky had become dislodged and come out. "Yea, he's free!" The man pulled himself up and staggered to Davey's voice and slid again into the culvert on the other side. He grabbed his son's body and pushed it up on to the bank. Davey shook in fear as he saw the boy all purple and still. The man pushed at his son's chest and roared, "Come back!" Davey's mom drove up in the battered station wagon, home from her nursing shift at the county hospital. She jumped from the car, pushed Ricky's dad away and began resuscitation. Ricky breathed. She looked over at her son and smiled.

A dog sniffed Davey's cheek, waking him up in a cold junky sweat. He got up with a groan, picking a blade of grass, remembering Eliot, let us go then, you and I. He chewed on the blade, stared at the birds, the clouds and the sky and walked off across the park. He set course for the cracked house.

His head throbbed as he came out of the alley directly across from the demonstration. The clamor played out in front of him.

He saw Jan and Gerard, yelling up at a wrecking-ball crane operator.

He let his right fist loose and his junk works fell to the ground.

He looked up at a KLM plane taking off from Schipol.

He saw Marion's flag, waving from the window.

He heard music in the air, the screech of Jimi Hendrix's riffing on the star spangled banner, hanging over the scene like a Van Gogh self-portrait.

He saw a small boy, running, running until he was out of breath.

Hawkbite

By Angelo Budoia

EXT BLUE SKY – DAY
Hawk flies high over ridgeline. Characters see hawk from different POV's.

EXT CLIFF LEDGE

JOHN "DUSTY" RENDON sees hawk upon awakening.

EXT RIDGETOP

CIELO Apache brave and former cavalry scout sees hawk from his horse.

EXT IN VALLEY

PETE RENDON Dusty's estranged brother, finishes lunch with his son, BLAINE, on the porch of their cabin. They watch hawk fly over ridge.

CLOSE ON BLAINE turning from the sky.

BLAINE
I... I don't want to leave here, daddy.

PETE

Don't you worry, Blaine. We're lucky; we have a place to go. Most people around here carry a big burden. They've got what you're grandpa used to call the "hawkbite." They got it so bad that they don't even know what they're doing anymore.

BLAINE

Why they keep trying, then?

PETE

Most of them are just numb, from all the fighting, all the traveling, all the struggling.

BLAINE

Like us, huh.

PETE

Not exactly, son. We've got options. I can go back east and work for the government and you can get a proper education and a more civil upbringing.

BLAINE

You sure it's not because mom's gone. I like it out here.

PETE

It's just that. I'm weary of it all. All these frontier fools running around.

BLAINE

You and Mrs.Seymour have done so much for everybody around here. The folks here need you.

                    PETE

I told Wendy about our intentions last night. You've got to give up
your concerns.

                    BLAINE

These are not my intentions, no. We got to make things come out all
right, right here.

                    PETE

Son, it'll all work out. I promise.

Blaine walks away, shaking his head. He looks up at the sky and then
back at Pete. Blaine goes up over a rise to a creek where he skips rocks
as he wades downstream.

EXT CREEK
A stone thuds sharply into the water.

CLOSE ON BLAINE
He grunts disapproval at the toss and carefully picks up another stone.
He positions himself and lets it fly.

EXT CREEK
The stone skips 1, 2, 3 ... times.

CLOSE ON BLAINE
A big grin is muffled by a blue clothed arm wrapping itself around his
head.

EXT CREEK
We see Blaine struggling as he is dragged across the creek into the trees
by Cielo.
We see the hawk fly off over the mountain.

EXT RANCH HOUSE
The Rocking S, one of the largest cattle ranches in the territory. We see two girls,
SHANA (13) and STEPHANIE (11), skipping rope out front as we go inside.

INT RANCH LIVING ROOM
Three characters, having coffee. WENDY SEYMOUR (33), divorced owner of ranch, vivacious, headstrong cowgirl and successful businesswoman. PABLO REA (60), ranch foreman. JOHN LEE (40), doctor.

PABLO

What now, Wendy, with Pete bent on leavin town and the territorial convention bein only three days off and Atchley's boys putting out all kinds of rancid rumors?

DR. LEE

Sure seems funny that Pete wants to leave now. I mean he's the one who brought us all together, helped us organize and stand up to Atchley.

WENDY

Misses the comforts back east? Who knows? His head wants to go.

DR. LEE

His head! What about our survival!

WENDY

Hell, Pete Rendon don't owe us a damn thing. We owe him.

PABLO

But, he promised...

WENDY

Never mind, that was yesterday. Sure, we need him and his connections. So, we're gonna offer him a cake that he can eat.

DR. LEE

You can't force him to stay, Mrs. Seymour.

WENDY

Dr. Lee, Pablo, Mr. Pete Rendon is going to be New Mexico Territory's next representative to Washington! Let's go see the man!

EXT VALLEY
Dusty Rendon rides through the trees.

EXT TOWN
Townspeople busy themselves preparing for Territorial Convention. Banners and posters are being tacked up. Hawkers set up their wares. People gather in groups arguing. An intense but festive atmosphere as we enter:

INT SHERIFF'S OFFICE
MAYOR GILLIAM AND SHERIFF SALCIDO sit around desk. The wall is covered with wanted posters, including one of "Dusty Rendon, Murderer."

SHERIFF

So, Atchley wants me to stir something else up against Mrs. Seymour and her delegation.

MAYOR

Listen sheriff, if she gets her people elected, you'll be back in the dirt with a pick in your hand.

SHERIFF
I'm just sick of doin Atchley's spade work!

MAYOR
If that woman hadn't dumped Atchley out of their marital bed and taken over her father's ranch, none of this would be happening. She's got to be stopped!

SHERIFF
I do believe you got a hankerin for her yourself.

EXT VALLEY
Dusty rides out of the trees to his brother's farm.

EXT BARN
Dusty approaches barn. He sees a body on the ground and dismounts with his canteen.
He recognizes the man as his brother.

TWO SHOT
Dusty kneels and Pete tries to speak.

DUSTY
Easy. Here. Drink.

PETE
Uh...Blaine...Blaine

DUSTY
Pete, it's me, Johnny...

PETE
Johnny!

DUSTY

Gawd...heard you were out this way, been a long time...sorry, sorry...

PETE

Find Blaine, find Blaine Johnny...

DUSTY

Who did this, Pete!

PETE

Never saw...never saw (looks to sky and gasps)...Blaine!
Pete succumbs. Tears wash Dusty's face.

FROM BEHIND

WENDY

Turn around slow, mister!

Dusty turns head to see Wendy, Pablo and Dr. Lee, with their rifles pointed at him.

EXT SHERIFF'S OFFICE
Four cavalry men in blue ride up and go inside.

EXT INDIAN CAMP
Cielo talks with Blaine. Twenty tribe members, mostly women and children, hover around a campfire.

BLAINE

Why would they kill him...why!

CIELO

They have killed many of my own...it is the work of their leaders...to take, to kill.

BLAINE

Why didn't you stop them?

CIELO

I was too late...all I could do was grab you away.

BLAINE

I guess I ought to thank you.

CIELO

No need. We must go soon. Where to take you?

INT SHERIFF'S OFFICE
Cavalry CAPTAIN GRAVES stands with his men behind him, talking to Mayor and Sheriff.

GRAVES

Atchley sent me. The rest of the detachment won't be here 'till tomorrow to monitor the convention activities. I persuaded the major to send us ahead, to scout out the countryside, been talk that the Apache Kid's been seen in these parts...

SHERIFF

Haven't heard that, Captain. Last report I had said he was 600 miles away, over in Arizona Territory.

One of the cavalry men (SHIELDS) scans the wall of wanted posters.

GRAVES

You probably don't get out much, do you Sheriff!

SHERIFF

(Gestures to Grave's bloodied sleeve) Not as much as you, I reckon!

GRAVES

Listen, you gob of spit! Atchley, our next territorial representative arrives tonight and I'm in charge. You stay put! My men will be goin out early in the morning, maybe there's some bad news will be arriving (wheels to leave), bad news for Mrs. Seymour (laughs), everyone knows no woman can protect us from these wild injuns (turns to door). I'll be at the hotel, or the saloon, if ya need me!

TWO SHOT

MAYOR

See, Sheriff, you got all upset for nothing. You won't have to worry about dirtying your hands anymore.

SHERIFF

Nothin. Nothin means anything you want for you and Atchley. Get outta my office.

EXT ROCKING S AT SUNSET

INT RANCH HOUSE

Dusty and Wendy in kitchen preparing to leave to search for Blaine. Shana and Stephanie at table eating.

WENDY

Finish up, girls.

SHANA

He sure looks like Pete, mama, except for his long hair, and he doesn't wear glasses.

WENDY

You're right on that one. Now, give us a kiss, honey.

The girls give Wendy hugs and kisses. Shana is embarrassed to kiss Dusty, but Stephanie manages a peck on his cheek. They go off to bed.

WENDY

They like you Johnny.

DUSTY

Thanks for callin me Johnny. It reminds me of a long time ago. Nice girls. Been a tough afternoon for them. I haven't had much time for family. Guess that's why I must have been trying to find Pete. Not so sure we should have buried him on your ranch. Blaine might not like it, if we can find him.

WENDY

We'll go as soon as Pablo gets back. I think Atchley's behind Pete's murder. I have a feeling that hiding the body here will force his hand. We can move him home later. We've got to trust each other, Johnny.

DUSTY

I appreciate you believing in me, Mrs. Seymour, but once we find Blaine, I gotta go.

WENDY

Go where? Blaine is your family. You said you wanted to stop running. Now's your chance.

DUSTY

I'm a wanted man.

WENDY

Yes you are. We want you to help us.

DUSTY

How?

WENDY

We were going to ask Pete to run for territorial representative. Atchley would kill me if I ran. Now, I'm going to ask you to take Pete's place, as his twin brother Johnny.

INT TOWN SALOON - SAME NIGHT
Large saloon with dance hall stage flanked by a raised tier of box seats on either side.
LORRAINE LADOW, singer/actress, belts out a tune to a capacity house.

TABLE NEAR STAGE
Seated are Graves, Mayor Gilliam and ATCHLEY (50), mustachioed land baron and Wendy's ex-husband.

ATCHLEY

I'm glad it's done, but this woman won't stop. She'll find some other man or even run herself. She knows too much.

GRAVES

Maybe the Apache Kid finds 'em and leaves 'em all dead.

MAYOR

Don't think we need that big a ruse. We got Cielo and his filthy

Apaches just out over the ridge. They're angry. We can pin it on them just like that.

ATCHLEY

Washington calls.

LORRAINE ON STAGE

LORRAINE

(To applause) Thank you, thanks one and all and don't forget the play tomorrow night. Your last chance to see some real actors, before those politicians start their babble on convention day!

Guffaws and cheers and applause. Lorraine steps off stage and takes Atchley's outstretched hand.

EXT RANCH HOUSE

Cielo lifts Blaine off of his horse.

CIELO

Cast your teeth to the sun...boy...

BLAINE

Good luck, Cielo...I hope you find the others in Sonora...

Cielo rides off.

INT RANCH HOUSE

Dusty and Wendy prepare their packs in the living room as Blaine bursts through the front door. Blaine eyes Dusty.

WENDY

Blaine, this is your Uncle Johnny, better known as Dusty Rendon. Dusty extends his hand. Blaine stares at him.

EXT RANCH VERRANDA
Dusty and Wendy on swinging couch.

WENDY

No, I don't think Pete really wanted to go away. Oh, that representative job would have been so right for him. He could have divided his time between here and Washington. He liked the land here, loved the light.

DUSTY

Strange how you get killed by trying to be decent folk, and me, I end up killing people because they want to kill me because they think I'm a killer. Makes no sense.

WENDY

You've had no choice, Johnny. You've had to defend yourself against senseless attacks, just like I have to do with Atchley. Let's hang in together and fight this thing.

DUSTY

I'll try it on.

WENDY

Maybe you can finally clear yourself.

DUSTY

Maybe...I wish I could have met a woman like you...before this train left...

WENDY

You met one now.

EXT TOWN STOCKYARDS/LIVERY – DAWN NEXT DAY
Graves enters with his three men. Pablo recedes behind a stall.

GRAVES
Bring the body back to the sheriff's office. Make a display of it. Bring the boy, too.

SHIELDS
Can't we leave the boy out of this?

GRAVES
You gettin clammy, Shields. Bring me both bodies! Now move!

Angelo ripped the page from his typewriter, stubbed his cigarette out in the Club 21 ashtray and gulped down the rest of his scotch on the rocks. He couldn't write this western claptrap for the series anymore. Enough, he thought. He had always wanted to write literature, to become a really fine novelist, not a television schlock. He had been sucked into the lure of Hollywood. I'm a hack, he thought, and a sellout. He rose up from his worn wooden chair and walked light headedly towards the side door and out into a patch of moonlight amidst the tall pines of his Topanga Canyon hideaway.

The fall of the great hawk was fast and sure, striking him in the neck and swiping him back up into the sky with a burst of the eight foot long wingspan, with the grope of the enormous weight of the man and a loud squawk and flap, higher and higher towards the full moon.

Dreams of a Ball in Flight

Hole 1. Ripper Springs Golf Course. Par 5, 490 yards. "Breakneck." Sharp dogleg left. Uphill. Steep ravine up entire left side. Two traps on left at 230 and 255 yards out. Green perched at end of crevice, pitched front to back with small shelf on back left.

Time ran out. What could Paul Spankleton say, to move them past what appeared to be the end. He crushed the words on the paper in his fist and let it fall, on Poanna's feet.

"Silly game," she said and put her hand on his shoulders to catch his eyes. She knew the heft of what he was trying to do. She knew that the 9th Annual Jumping Cholla Golf Tournament would not provide a winner as usual.

"Silly game," he said.

"It's the now or never thing," she said, "This will help the jet-lag." She poured his first cup of coffee and strolled across the veranda into the clubhouse, turning to him as if to say - finish, Spanky.

He hung his legs off the stone wall that held the terrace to the hillside, in the shade of the palm thatched ramada, past the small infinity pool, and gazed out toward the pier that jutted into the bay at the same angle that the 200 foot cliff pawed its way from northeast to southwest, into the Sea of Cortez. The local fishermen from El Jardin used the pier to tie up to during severe storms. He watched Kicker and Ky, his daughter and Po's son, both in their early twenties now, akimbo at the end of the wooden planks. They made up dives, solo and together, hand-in-hand, screaming with piercing laughs into the sea, like the hell-diving cormorants doing the same thing from even greater heights. As he watched them fly, Spanky felt the water well from the wrinkles at the corners of his eyes.

Hole 2. Par 3, 195 yards. "Windnface." Back down ravine southwest towards sea. Green sits alone on edge of cliff. Kidney shaped green with one large pot bunker front left. Wildgrass and catclaw surround slopes of green.

The flight to Caracas had been smooth, except for the constant nervous banter of his two old friends, Oaf and Frus. The big men often served as his bodyguards, companions and visceral associates. They were full of tales of their warriorhood. He and Blue, his metaphysical advisor, sat facing each other, exchanging occasional notes and nods towards the men across the aisle. They were to be met by J.D. Grandbois, his business partner for over 30 years. Instead they were met by machine guns in their bellies and a directive to enter President Torreo's hangar. They stood in front of a long table and Spanky recognized the faces of the men who ruled the world, the men that he had played off of for years and had always maintained an edge over. J.D. sat next to Don Martin Jimenez, the most powerful drug lord on earth. Don Martin stood.

"Welcome, Mr. Spankleton. For years you have attempted to exercise financial control over the competing forces in the world's economy through your implementation of the fusion process. Now you have tried to have your Mr. Grandbois have us believe that it would be to our advantage to turn in all of our out of market cash into the market with a fifty percent tax from our various countries, and replace our drug crops with legitimate ones." Don Martin spoke calmly. Grandbois would not look at Spanky. "This would be good," he continued, "If good is what we wanted. Fairness and balance, as you well know, are not what we value. The well being of the hordes is not our concern. Your vision has been our loss. The corporate collectives and the black market collectives gathered here both agree on this. We have seized all of your processing sites. We will dismantle them. We don't want them. We will return to the old ways of oil wells, nuclear fission reactors, mota, coca and poppies. Mr. Grandbois has kindly prepared all of the paperwork necessary for the transfer of all your assets to Reesabank, my holding company. We will also be moving our prime base of operations to your enclave near El Jardin. In exchange, you and your friends may live. Mr. Grandbois will work for me. You have ten days to vacate your Ripper Springs."

Forced relinquishment. Spanky faced Blue as the Gulfstream X streaked back home into the sunset across the Gulf of Mexico.

"We've got to evacuate everyone immediately, give them a chance to live out their lives," said Spanky.

"What about the tournament," said Blue.

"You're kidding. We've got to call it off."

"No way, brah. It's the only choice left."

"Bullshit. The deadline for the takeover is the day after the tourney ends. We'd never get out of there. We're fucked."

"You're not in charge anymore. We need a collective response to the takeover based on intensive acceleration of our past life lessons. The tournament will serve as a vehicle for our ultimate cellular transformation," said Blue.

"There's no way out, is there," said Spanky.

"There's only a way in," said Blue.

"Into what? The lords have it all now. So, what should I tell them?"

"You'll know."

Spanky knew that collapse and chaos were coming, that all would fall down. It was time for him to follow his life lesson. The stakes were high and the ability of his friends to comprehend their own lessons could open a window that would unkill language, pierce the illusion of separateness and wake the dead. They must collectively change the energy. Create a new past, present and future.

Hole 3. Par 4, 310 yards. "Flash." Runs north along cliff, 200 foot drop to rocky beach on left. Lush desert forest of blue agave and yucca borders 35 yard wide hug fairway on right. Green 30 feet wide and 80 feet long. Putting surface on edge of cliff to west and falls off steep slope to east into agave.

What to say, to move them past the utopian scene, to capture the fire within, to climb down the cliff to pick the rose from the hanging ledge, to change the world. Spanky's tiny Baja refuge had turned into a village like Honaunau, the ancient Hawaiian sanctuary on the Big Island of Hawaii. How appropriate, since the native Kona kahuna, Blue, had wandered in (wondered in is what Blue said he did), a year after Poanna. Blue had helped him put the last pieces of his life together through his ability to read and interpret past lives, rendering life lessons, forcing Spanky to confront his own. Now the lessons must be made manifest and joined, if there was to be any kind of real world.

They must collectively change the energy in their souls, suspended between the cliffs and the sea at Ripper Springs.

Hole 4. Par 4, 415 yards. "Pissfire." Straight up the mountain. Green tucked into rocky ledge and surrounded by rock wall, flecked with petroglyphs, where the ghosts of the living meet the ghosts of the dead.

Po was the first to have been drawn to Ripper Springs and the first thing she had said to him was, "This is the jumping off point." Then she said, "You need me and the others who will come." She leaned on him with her dark eyes and he was overcome with the feeling that he had become lost and found at the same time. He had managed to carve out an exotic, hidden world on the beach for himself and his friends, but Po's arrival confirmed that it would not hold. He was reminded of a song from his youth in Pleasant Valley, Arizona, "Weight's What Broke the Wagon Down," sung by the Wheels in three part harmony from the dimly lit corner stage of the Lightning Bar. He had assumed that he had the weight in balance when he had made nuclear fusion practical and held the process out as a way to regulate the world players and isolate with his kind in a paradise, far from the madding machinations of the new world order.

"It will take some time, but we need to begin to dream a new dream," she said, "one that will sustain and thrive without this need to hide." She had brought her young son, Ky, who got along well with his daughter, Kicker. Po helped him finish the golf course and the clubhouse and they built more casitas down the beach, for those to follow. She had told Spanky about her ex-husband and he realized that she wasn't done with the man. He was spooked when he realized that the man, Pepe, had also been his childhood best friend. Spanky, Po,

Blue and Pepe became partners in what was to unravel and unfold.

Hole 5. Par 4, 385 yeards. "Helpmerhonda." Follows a steppe high about the club and the bay. Out of a stone shoot, hole goes slightly right, following the bend of the rocky face on the left. Steep drop-off on right. Green is boomerang shaped, with nothing but air if missed short and right.

Spanky flinched from his reverie, late on that cloudy, windswept Sunday afternoon, wiped his eyes and quickly wrote the announcement. He stood and strolled toward some of the regulars who sat on the porch extending from the lounge overlooking the curl of the bay.

Oaf and Frus were there. Oso. Poanna. Marge. Billie. Flagstick. Blue. Errie. Paul and Sanjor. Scrounger. Pelon and Peggy. Blasé. Beasterfield. Betty. Mary Ann. Calvary. Pepe.

Paul Spankleton was "the man" for all of them - the finder, builder and founder of the golf club by the sea. A self-proclaimed inventor and world player, Paul was a seventy-two year old scientist, entrepreneur, steer wrestler, surfer, rambler, golfer and a cross-dresser of sorts. He liked to look like a Sikh from India, preferring violet to white robes, yet he always wore a loose muumuu around his beach-house. His constant companion was Sanjor Watt, a small, ruddy-faced man, with hooded eyes and a crooked smile, who spoke nonsense. Sometimes Paul also went by the name of Sanjor and was prone to say, "Everyone is a little sanjor." He also liked to be called "Spanky" and "Stick Horse," but hated it when he heard the name "Alfalfa" that Pepe had given him years ago, whispered behind his back.

The others had found him and the springs by the same sort of magnetic draw as Poanna - pulled in as acquiescent refugees from a world that seemed to have lost its sense.

Oaf leaned over on Frus's shoulder. "You better let go of trying to win the tourney, wonder man, it's all mine."

"Fuck off, you big oaf! You should do the let go part – let go of your rude on course interference – maybe I just might sink a putt if you weren't muttering in my backswing!"

"You're so damned frustrated that you'd grasp at absolutely anything to justify your incompetence!" said Oaf.

"Incontinence!" Hell, I got five kids," replied Frus.

Oaf and Frus went on, like they always went on. Both were big men who had big appetites for banter.

Spanky overheard them, howled as he passed by the giants and made his way around the room, table-hopping like a senator at work in the Capitol dining room.

"Quite fortunate," he said.

"What do you mean," said the two big men in unison.

"Quite fortunate that you're both not plugged in the face of life's bunker."

Sanjor smiled a half smile, and Spanky knew that all of their tales, all of their digging around would matter soon.

He continued his rounds, biting his tongue as he passed Pelon and Peggy.

"Why can't you see the golf ball as god?" said Pelon, rubbing his bald head.

"Well, I like my god with a little flesh on him!" said Peggy.

"A flesh golf ball?" asked Pelon.

"Why not - you know that Errie says that "thumb wrestling" is just another name for putting, so why not a pulsating flesh golf ball god?"

"That's just what I was saying."

Spanky looked around the room at all the regulars. He was always astonished at their physical diversity and the great range of their life stories, yet they had things in common. They had all been to the bottom and back, they could all hit a golf ball solidly and they had miraculously found this place. He never forced the others to get life readings from Blue. They all wanted one, out of curiosity, out of hunger. They all came to know each other's stories and lessons and often used this knowledge to make opportune verbal jabs on the links or in the lounge. Now they must dig into their lessons and find a way to play.

Hole 6. Par 3, 162 yards. "Rama." Ledge to ledge, across precipice to a half-moon green wedged between giant boulders.

He banged a fork on a glass. "Listen up. The tournament is the day after tomorrow. There will be no individual winner, but we must all strive for our lowest score and we must come to mastery of our life lessons by the end of the round. We must all come to this, for we do not know what lies beyond. Anyone who wants to leave now can do so, but all of my information points to immanent earthly annihilation of our species. The tipping point has been reached. Now we must create our own turning point."

Sanjor tugged on his sleeve. He leaned over for a whisper. "Sanjor wants to say a few words to you." Sanjor stands on a table.

"Framble as you amble. Sample the ample lookas and blooks, the assorted heavenly delights and fragrant rambling samples of heartswells in the night. With rolling cool fingers, go for the hilt. The eye in your belly knows all the ways and will refuse the right to reserve service to anyone. Clam diggers and fish pullers hold on to the day, for the fresh lake fish of men sometimes go astray. Enchanting whispers carry the choices, the wind inside unleashes the voices, the spot is their, in your rejoices."

Spanky jumped from the rock into the sand, wondering about the jumble of the words, laughing as he trudged down the beach, remembering when he first heard from Blue that his life lesson was discernment through chaos. But he soon realized that it had nothing to do with abundantly assessing the world, which he had done. No, it had to do with relinquishing control. He could now finally confront his need to possess a seeing spirit, which he certainly did not have in his past life, from which he must finally learn.

Hole 7. Par 4, 441 yards. "Cliffhanger." Cliff face going up on left. Cliff dropping off on right. This cut is 40 yards wide, with a big rock in the left center of the fairway at 260 yards. Green is arrowhead shaped and slopes severely from left to right.

Pepe stepped from the tight Bermuda fairway into the deep fescue and tall desert chaff. He stretched his arms in a high arc towards the deep blue sky and felt the bite of the strong ocean breeze. He was glad to be away from them all.

No place I'd rather be, he thought. Alone. Playing the game. No matter the insistent rub of it all – the endless search and frustration bound with the infusion of insight and the occasional moment of wondrous execution. The game kept winding within him and was the only game he had ever played where one might feel that everybody was watching, even when playing by oneself. A twisted game, he thought, the only antidote to this self-consciousness being self-invisibility.

What was it that scraped at his mind like the foul whispers of so many ex-wives? Was it women or Poanna in particular? Spanky's announcement about the upcoming tournament had left him full of dread. The Jumping Cholla Memorial had always honored Mortie, who, reeling drunk one night tumbled into a large clump of the nasty cactus, was severely poisoned, caught pneumonia, and died nine days later at the Red Cross over in El Jardin. Pepe tried to imagine what might have been going on during Mortie's last day, the day his resistance died.

Mortie saw the day of the dead man in the mirror. It was a great makeup job and matched his insides. He had found the club and thought it was his way out, but he just couldn't go with their ways, with what he saw as a pushing for him to change. He was exactly who he wanted to be. Skeleton, devil man with white sunken cheeks, nose less, wearing his dad's old pork pie hat and long rain coat, Levi's and boots. His eyes were red and peered back at him with a deadness that almost startled.

He fumbled for his vial and poured a big pinch of the glistening powder onto the fleshy seam at the bottom of his thumb, the way his grandpa Maynard had done snuff. The quick snort went straight away through his third eye deep into the gray matter, short-circuiting the pathways, taking over even the numbness of his afternoon of drinking on the couch. Back to the clubhouse party now, for another double scotch from the bar, back to lurid meandering amidst the others, costumed in all manners on the hallowed eve. He groped, stumbled and spattered, vaguely sensing their repulsion. Unable to speak, he felt the urge, stumbled outside, doggedly into the stillness of the desert air, tottered over the short wall and weaved his way amidst the cholla forest at the edge of the ravine. He found a spot to go and unzipped his pants, only aware of his heaviness, seasick in the silence of his breath. The stars were painted into the black void and he felt only foreign and ashamed, only a glint of who he was remained and he had no name.

He peed hard as a horse, trying to force years of the dreaded cycle from his tumescent veins, zipped up and staggered, overcome by lightheadedness and was seized, toppled backwards, to his right side, into the joints of a huge section of jumping cholla. He tried to break his fall with the back of his right hand, arm and shoulder, but they caught a mass of thistle-white needles, which plunged and plugged into his moaning body as it hit the ground. All was quiet again, after the tumult and shout.

He saw so much of himself in Mortie, had the same case, that of a slammed down man. He had vowed at the funeral to win, win it for Mortie and their mutual salvation. For three years running the bronze cactus cup had been snatched from his grasp by Poanna herself. Now this would be the last tournament and there would be nor more champions of the Ripper Springs Club. Somehow he had slipped the bonds of booze, but not of Mortie, nor of his own answer to the question of what gives, what must give? Mortie had been his best friend back in the Portal days and had spent many hours with him and Poanna, before she had left Pepe and found her way to the compound. Poanna and her dreams. He reached into his wallet and unfolded her crumpled poem.

> The dawn seekers stir
> From the sleepy shadow
> Open eyes wide
> To a crimson sky
> Punctured by the bruised void
> Of the mountain god
> On Babaquivari.
> Shafts of light pierce
> Their hearts, unfolding
> To receive soft hits
> Of whisking rain
> Sounding reveille.

Pepe winced. How could such poetic thoughts later turn into a piercing look and voice that said, "Pass the fucking ketchup!" Estranged for years and now somehow back in the same place, she still continued to drive his mind to the brink and she still throttled him on the links like she was beating a large pow-wow drum.

"Pepe, what the hell you doin," said Poanna.

Silent earth mingles,
Shoots through the feet
Flowing upward to release
In sharp morning tears.
The bodies rise from a bed
Of lupine and wild grass,
Mesmerized beyond dreams,
Floating in the draft,
Drifting high above
The enchanted isles
Through spangled rays
Into the rolling clouds.

He looked up at her standing on top of the slope, behind the tee, her black hair flying into the blue void. She had caught up with him and found him sitting on the edge of the tee-box, staring up at the mountain.

The destined creatures
Huddle in the spiral shroud,
Shields on the silent songs
Fall off and penetrate the calm.
Out of sleep they snap awake,
Hearing horses clapping down.
The man with no attitude
Now has a seed,
Sown in the love rain,
Nourished by the dream.

"Reading your poem, the one you wrote for us back in Portal."

"Get over it. You've been down there for ten minutes. It's been like watching a wounded animal, for christsakes!"

They ascend to the first day,
Beyond the pall,

Their faces open
Along the lines of life,
The hearts flash
Under the lights.
Under the lights
Without wings they fall
In a clear watery bead,
To share chosen moments
On the shore of the well
Of much remembering.

"So, what happened to the *you* who wrote this poem?" he said.
"The poem, it's about golf, not us!" she said.

They dwell close
In the curl of the green wave
Lit up by the shine of the
Starwave.
A rainbow is cast
In the corner of their eyes.
Crackling sea bubbles
Rub the bellies
Of the ocean inside.
Bright silver threads
Push out from the center,
Tangling the riders
Inside out as they enter
Starwave.

"Bullshit, why don't you want to talk about us?"

Wrapped up in the spray
Of sparkle and cry,
The long rolling crash
Upside down and under
The embrace gives
Way to thunder.

"Us! Don't you see? It's now about all of us; we've got to try to move beyond it all. This is our only real chance."

In the long foaming fuse,
Breaking apart
Between terror and wonder
Only to join with smile and laugh
In the delta of undertow clash.

"Chance to what? It's all over, don't you see. The last gasp tournament thing is a fool's game. I can't do Spanky's bidding any more. I say let's go. You and me, let's take off into the heart of Mexico. Screw Spanky and Blue and the rest. Maybe it's all about our love for each other."

"Spanky's got it right," she said, "We're all headed down the rabbit hole."

"There's still time to get out," he said.

"No, we've come this far and we've got to see it through," she said.

"Go on then, go, I need to practice by myself."

She disappeared from his view, slipping over to the 14th hole. He slumped back on his spine on the soft grass like a roll of carpet being kicked open. Her smell lingered and he thought of that bright morning near Portal.

Hole 8. Par 3, 215 yards. "The Weight." 80 foot drop off ledge over large, tumbled rock escarpment to large, two-tiered green. All carry. Surrounded on three sides by cholla cactus.

He had been hiking up Cave Creek, following the glint of the sun off the water, headed toward the falls, when he first saw her mid-air jumping from rock to rock in the middle of the stream. He leaped towards the top of a wet boulder and slid off into a dark pool. She turned when she heard his wail as he emerged from the cold froth. She bounded back towards him, flying across the rocks. "Are you okay?" He was caught by her deep blue eyes as he struggled back on to the rock. They began to laugh together, laughed so hard that the pine needles seemed to sway along the creek bank. Out of this moment sprang the most mysterious and powerful force on earth, a child. Within a year they had their son Ky who brought them expanded light.

Where did it all go? He wanted her now, more than he wanted her then. *If I can't have her, though, at least I can beat her, the hell with all the rest of it.* He couldn't even think about the rest of it, about Spanky's plan and what was to come. Pepe knew he must focus on the game and take the title, even if it was his last thing - if he could just stop beating himself and find his way from the fishbowl to the stream and somehow get her back.

Hole 9. Par 5, 585 yards. "Diver." Sharp dogleg left down the mountain toward the clubhouse.

Pepe rolled backwards up into a stance, addressed the ball and flailed at his drive. He walked head down in the rough grass along the wash that ran along the left side of the 13th hole, down towards the springs and the oasis of mesquite, willow and palm that hugged the warm pond and the narrow green of the par five, where he had hit the pull, over-the-top, snipe hook. He slipped down the slope on to the sand and rocks. His white golf shoes were submerged in the flowing water of the arroyo, fresh from the morning chubasco dumped on the rocky outcroppings of Coyote Peak that sheltered the springs and the small bay from occasional fierce Pacific storms tracking north up the coast from their tropical source.

Pepe had climbed the peak many times. Spanky had shown him the hidden trail, behind the giant granite boulder, that led up the gorge to the ridge of the "old ones." They had camped in the cave hung in the cliff laden with the scars of the ancient artists and seers who had carved images of scorpion, antelope, javelina, wildcat, man and maze into the rose colored walls. Spanky always said that we "caliche colored ones" hadn't even begun to learn from these scratched gifts. During one distant sunrise, with rainbow colors on it, Pepe had sensed the underlying spirit of all beings, there in the crevice, under the peak, in a misty fog, in the form of a shiver that raised the hair on his arms and the fizzed the cells in his brain.

The memories brought him to a stop. That certainty of source had since been shaken, stripped, restored, and replaced by the resistance and confusion that he now felt, and it was not due to Poanna or

Spanky's announcement. He looked up and followed a hawk as it rode a thermal across the face of the cliffs and out to sea, looked down at the rocks in the wash, at the glistening quartz and the odd round object, half submerged in the waters flow. He feared that nothing would relieve his misfortune, but he knew better, had run up against it before. Part victim, he felt, part creator of the grist of his own unraveling fate. What next, what next. He chose the wedge and carefully rocked his feet into a stance.

He had come to love trouble shots. In the past, in a solo practice round, he would have merely hit another ball from the fairway rather than scramble down the side of the wash. Not since Blue had come to the club, though. The Hawaiian had given him and the others a different way of seeing, not unlike the ancient ones from the peak above, but it was somehow disturbing, a loss through forever learning something true. Now was the time to deal with the forces within that seemed to oppose his very existence.

Blue had to stir it all up, Pepe thought, as he dug into the rocky slush. The horse's ass chose to confront their comfort and their complacency. It was during his first session with him that Pepe began sensing how precarious his life was, how utterly without control. All of this began with a life reading and parting comment by the kahuna. "Balance the notions with the motions, Pepe. Find quality, that is your lesson." Pepe didn't want that in his ears. No, he could control his own destiny and Blue could take his preposterous suppositions, admonitions and revelations and shove them up his ass!

Thwack! A powerful swing. Flushed up fat, the white ellipse floated out in a muddy spray of gravel, flew to the top of the embankment, and tumbled back down to his feet. Same shot all over again. It seemed that he was frequently starting over, ever since Blue had sat him down and started in with his past life story, Pepe's affecting life, Blue called it, an opportunity to meet himself. Pepe didn't like what he heard, yet knew he must change, that he had never had power over the mundane, that the elusive quest for love, meaning and redemption was about to begin, again, in earnest.

Hole 10. Par 4, 324 yards. "De Nada." Back up mountain. Narrow fairway to a small, convex green.

Ky burst through the screen door of Poanna's ocean bungalow. "How can you just give in like this," he said.

Poanna sat draped over her favorite oversized bamboo deck chair, looking out past Pelican Island. She had finished her practice round, had a lesson from Errie and was unwinding. It was just like her son to be so dramatic. With the dancing chromosomes from her and Pepe, he had no choice.

"No one is giving in, son," she said, "We're giving it up."

"You don't get it," said Ky. "It's all a ruse. Blue is bullshit, through and through. Look at this."

Hole 11. Par 4, 410 yards. "Chaos." Sharp dogleg right along ridge and over chasm fronting green.

Errie hated working with Spanky. His blithe unconcern permeated the air between them. Erie called him "Smug in the mug." Spanky called him "Almighty Fixer." Yet Erie knew what kept bringing him back. It was his intrigue with the ball in flight. This is what kept them all coming back - the unexpected identification, push, pull and release into thin air of a ball struck in the center of the clubface. All aspects of the game could become excruciating. Spanky called it "The Relentless Pursuit of Sysyphus." Yet not one of them could deny the shear ethereal delight of the flying of the ball.

"Assume the position," said Errie, thus initiating the dreaded regimen of practice that he demanded of his pupils. Spanky eyed him for a moment, then lay on his back and rocked his legs back over his torso - one, two, three - nine times. Always sets of nine. The yoga like practice continued out under the shade of a giant Ironwood tree, blooming now with what seemed gobs of pink popcorn hanging from the faint green leaves. The practice area was up above the mesquite bosque, to the right of the first hole. There were three holdable greens at 100, 150 and 180 yards and a small practice green with a sand bunker to the side of the range. There was a lone yucca valida at the top of the rise at 290 uphill. No one had ever reached it. Spanky continued his stretches for about thirty minutes. Then he and Erie did some Tai Chi, with each of them holding a golf club between their hands. Spanky always liked this part, although he would never let on. He hit one more driver. It flew over the top of the yucca.

"Good luck, tomorrow," said Errie.

Spanky smiled as he walked away, glad that Errie put him through a normal practice session with so much really on the line. He let go as the sun set over the Baja sea like an orange meat ball.

Hole 12. Par 3, 171 yards. "Rumi." All carry over rock mesa to green surrounded by sand bunkers.

"No, we do nothing," said Poanna as she passed Blue's tattered diary back to Ky.

"He may be a liar, but he speaks the truth. We will all go down into the blackness at the bottom of the cup." They hugged and looked up to the star fires glowing in the darkness.

Hole 13. Par 5, 568 yards. "Steamer." Back down to the sea. Mineral pools shared with the 18th hole, behind green that slopes from front to back.

Blue had seen the rosy fingered dawn more than once. He had come into this life with only one lesson: follow the shaft of light. Although he had lied to them about his past life, it was because they wouldn't have understood. He knew that the past, present and future hung in the balance and that the tournament would lead to free flight and final escape from the wheel of earthly dharma, that it would be the keyhole to the white light. He cleaned his clubs with a wet towel, sat down and pulled on his golf shoes.

Hole 14. Par 4. 280 yards. "Pass the Apocalypse." Driveable with a 260 yard carry over the sea.

The 9th Annual Jumping Cholla Golf Tournament started with the squack from Spanky's airhorn. The shotgun start would enable the ten twosomes to finish at just about the same time.

Po started steadily, paring the first 7 holes. Then she birdied two in a row, putting her in the lead at the halfway point. She took great satisfaction in informing Pepe with the words "You're still away," on the 6th green, after his approach putts had sailed far past the hole. Sanjor scurried around the course in a golf cart, reporting everyone's progress to each group via updated text messages.

Hole 15. Par 4. 390 yards. "Tiltawhirl." Uphill to small green perched on cliff ledge.

POANNA TWO UNDER THROUGH 10. KY LIPS OUT FOR EAGLE ON 9TH HOLE, MUTTERS SOMETHING ABOUT FINALLY LEARNING HOW TO FLY. BLUE UNABLE TO CLIMB OUT OF RAVINE ON 5TH HOLE, FOLLOWS A SHAFT OF LIGHT BACK UP TO THE GREEN. OAF SUFFERS RUB OF THE GREEN ON 12TH TEE AS A GUST OF WIND CARRIES HIS BALL OVER THE GREEN, CAREENING IT OFF CLIFF, OUT OF BOUNDS. HE SAYS THAT HE GETS IT, THAT HE IS NOT IN CHARGE OF HIS FATE. SPANKY LOSES A BALL SOMEWHERE OFF OF 14TH FAIRWAY AND IS NOT PHASED. WITH THREE HOLES TO GO, THE LEADERS ARE: POANNA, 2 UNDER; SPANKY 1 UNDER; FLAGSTICK 1 UNDER; KY EVEN; OAF EVEN; PEPE 2 OVER; BLUE 4 OVER. SANJOR, FOREVER.

Hole 16. Par 3, 108 yards. "Olvidalo." A flip wedge down to desert spindle of earth, with nothing but air on down the cliffs on all sides of the green and a wooden bridge to get across from the ridge to the putting surface.

The cracks began to open up along the lines of their lives. The great unlocking manifests physically in the earth as they approach the end of their rounds. They are not fully aware of their participation in this awakening. Poanna and Pepe have completed their round, with Poanna in the lead at 2 under par. They walk hand in hand back down the hill to the hot spring at the side of the 18th hole, with Pepe understanding that he will never beat Poanna and now knowing it is not important. They take off their shoes and socks and dangle their feet in the warm water, embracing each other and watching the rest of the field come down the fairway, all lessons learned, following the last group to finish, Flagstick and Spanky. They notice the water in the spring becoming hotter.

Out in the fairway, Spanky picks a 3 iron and surveys his second shot into the par 5. He could see Poanna and Pepe entwined on the far bank of the steaming spring. He looks back, up towards the tee and notices that the ravine that they had just crossed was opening wider and emanating a rich molten light. There is a party atmosphere in the small crowd as Spanky addresses his shot and puts a mighty swing on the ball, catching it flush and sending it high, towards the final pin.

Hole 17. Par 4. 423 yards. "Free Flight." Roundhouse hole follows the cliff. Bite off as much as you can chew.

All eyes fix on the ball as it reaches its apex and vanishes. Poanna and Pepe strain to find the ball in a sky that has turned a brilliant gold as the earth cracks apart in a thousand lines, like a shattered window, releasing white light and enfolding the firmament. The moment is lit with this firelight and all is determined through the glow. They all are free to go. Then, now and forever.

Hole 18. Par 5. 522 yards. "On the Beach." Downhill to home.

Poanna and Pepe walk through the thick jungle growth and come to a black sand beach that leads to a silver sea with two suns setting on a horizon producing rich violet rays. They leave their footprints in the sand as they run towards the water. Pepe stops and points to a funny little object near the waterline. It's a little white ball with dimples in it. He picks it up and tries to bite it. Poanna laughs and grabs a long piece of bleached driftwood with a knob on the end. She gestures for Spanky to throw the ball down. She steps towards the ball and swings the stick, striking the ball up into a long arc out over the ocean towards the suns falling away into the void.

Forever finding
The way of the waves,
Nurturing the grace
Of the fire dancing free.
White caps breaking
Over the edge of the sun,

Exposing hearts,
Leaving no one undone.
The cloud is moving,
Changing form in the dawn,
Turning into the hand of god
And is gone...

2061

Old Ky pulled on his earlobe. The tick had been with him for most of his eighty two years. He sat in stillness. He waited for nightfall on the porch of his grandson Jason's house, facing west/northwest, the direction of the rise of Halley's Comet. He had seen her before, in the fall of 1986, when he was seven, perched on his father's shoulders, facing up, west/northwest.

"What?" said Ky.

Jason pushed open the screen door, "You alright, grandpa?" He saw him nod and he went back inside. The twilight turned Ky's face a deep orange.

"Follow..."

"What?" He said.

Jason came out again. He went over and put his hand on Ky's shoulder. Ky responded by covering his grandson's hand with his own, his free hand cradling the manuscript in his lap.

"You'll be able to see it soon, grandpa." Jason pushed the post of the rocking chair forward, gently setting the old man in motion.

•

Young Ky heard the call of his father, "Finish the game, son, we got to get home for the comet party."

Ky loved the arcade. He would spend hours playing all the electronic games. His favorites were the new role-playing games, which allowed him to follow clues and make choices. Of these, he most often played Future Now, an electronic game that dispensed philosophical tidbits and thoughts of wonder when he maneuvered the game's hero through various predicaments. He called the new insights he gained "dreamballs." They formed the basis for his later inquiries into synchronicity and human flight.

In the car, his dad said, "You know, if you play your cards right and understand your lesson and you want to - you just might be able to seen Halley when she returns again in seventy five years." They both had what his dad called a "wishbone chuckle" on that one. His father was a teacher, his grandfather a train engineer. They had freed each other in succession as generations are wont. For Ky, it was to pursue what had meaning, pushing him to his innermost core, to the lesson of what was true and real and full of wonder. It was science and art, all wrapped up in one big ball of string. His art was his passion and had made him rich and famous. The game of golf was his life practice, his humorous obsession. Finally he wrote it down, the why of it all. His book sat in his lap now.

•

Jason pushed again on Ky's chair. He recalled the old man's immense accomplishments, his sense of enthusiasm for life - for keeping after his dreams, for seeing the sacred in the profane, for the peace and quality he so freely gave away. He rocked him in the old blue rocker until the darkness set in.

•

Young Ky saw it first. "There it is, dad - jeez, I'll bet the tail is a million miles long!"

"And a million more," said his dad.

•

"There she is, grandpa! See!" Jason pointed over Ky's shoulder toward the light. He knew from all the stories how much it meant to him to have made it to this day.

Ky saw the faint white glow, like the head of an extinguished match, arched like a ball in flight. He strained to see more, peering back even into his past lives. He saw the deep blue eyes of a long past love, heard the comforting voice of a father on a camping trip and the faint echo of a baby crying, felt the soft skin of a young girl in Amsterdam, followed the pulse of a mineral rod and the vibration of a hawk in flight, and played golf in the splendor of a Baja paradise.

The light seemed to grow brighter.

Jason rocked him for a few more minutes.

THE NINETEENTH HOLE

Addenda and Acknowledgements

"There are only three principles to remember in the game:
Impeccability, resiliency and invisibility." Errie Low

UP FRONT

(Being a letter written by my father to my mother during World War II)

Somewhere in Italy
3 November 1943
Marge, My darling,

A m trying to make up for not getting my regular letters off the other day when I went on the island trip - so will try and tell you something about it. Six of us have been hoping to do just such an adventure for the past two months - Buddy H. - from Shreveport; Dan H., my anesthesiologist from Chicago; Jim H. and Alex R. from Tenn. - and small town boys on top of that. Charlie S. from some small Ill. town. We started out in a jeep and after driving (in various cramped positions) for several hours, we reached the beautiful little town of Sorrento which is on the peninsula across from the Isle of Capri.

Due to its geographic location this town has been little tarnished either by fighting or occupation by troops - tho some wander around the streets, shopping leisurely in sunny Italy, when it isn't raining as it was the day I arrived there. It was here that I met the delightful little boy Tony when his father hired on as our guide and arranged lunch and transportation for us.

A boat was finally procured to take us over for $30. So we rounded up ten other passengers in town to ride along and share expenses as a matter of fact. Altho the distance was short - around three miles - it took us an hour and a half on this 25 footer, with a one cylinder motor and sails with holes in them - to come into the small harbor of the island. The island itself is small with cliffs at each end and a valley between. It noways compares with the beauty of Catalina Harbor in its natural composition. However, its history, buildings, people and customs, coupled with its present nearness to the battle front amazes such a tourist as I am.

Upon arriving there an electric cable car took us up to the town – all of which reminded me of San Francisco and how much I'd like being back there with you – so I was quite ready for their idea of an American bar at the top of the hill. Liquor – by the drink – is plentiful there at 45 cents a thimble full – which I drank as fast as they could pour them out up to about a half pint. (It was White Horse Scotch but they had no others). Then we went to a very modern hotel – Dave and I shared a room and the balcony overlooking the harbor, beautiful Mediterranean, etc.

Food was next on our list of musts – tho I never got to far from the aforementioned bar – and we ended up feasting as I haven't done since I left the States – but we did pay happily for it all. I had steak and egg every meal for the two and a half days we were there. All this – I found out later – is bought thru black markets and the price is prohibitive for the natives there who eat practically nothing but potatoes and a cheap soup of some sort. Now that U.S. rations coming in – I do hope they will receive ample amounts and sure they will. I won't tell you – until later – how much these luxuries cost me, darling, for you would probably lose all incentive to save anything at all – but it was heavenly while it lasted. The only depressing part was not having you with me – but I did think and dream of you – to say nothing of longing for you all the time.

It is a very romantic spot – but probably more so in such times · and the people I met told such tales which cannot be written about but I'll tell you all of it later.

The boys all bought lots of presents etc. I bought you some typical purses and a small cap, also some souvenirs for the boys – the remainder of my money I loaned to Dave to buy a beautiful Prato Cameo Set – the only decent jewelry on the island. Everything else can be duplicated there at home at Woolworths.

We caught a boat at 6 A.M. our second morning there and came back to Sorrento – during which trip ole Vesuvius was beautiful with flames lighting up the skies. Once back to the car we loaded in and returned home, tired and hungry again – guess the G.I. food is pretty good after all – it's hardy and in abundance – tho plain.

Marge, my sweet, there is so much I would like to write you about, and it's so tough to weed out things I can't write and thus giving you an inkling of how things are. Am going up front again and probably won't have time to write other V-Mails for quite some time. I'll never get used to the big guns, plane strafing and bombing and always feel thankful to still be in one piece after getting to back to some peace and quiet. Our ground forces really have the toughest job as far as I can see in spite of what Jack says about the AirCorp. It's when I am in a clear state that I feel justified in being separated from you and Pat and Mike – and helping all that's possible to save some of these gallant soldiers who get wounded – have never seen one yet who had any gripes about doing his share.

There has never been a day or nite pass – since we parted – that I haven't spent hours thinking of you, wondering and worrying if your were all right and hoping and praying that you three will always be safe and happy and away from these miseries of war. That outweighs my selfish desires and longings to be with you for my pleasures and makes it possible to carry on until things are finished over here. So darling, if you grow even half as lonesome for me as I am for you remember we will make up for it all and more.

Please don't worry about my future but that of yours and Pat and Mike's and may all of you and your family be hopeful and happy. You may depend on me loving you more and more each day thinking of you more, praying for you more until we are together again my darling.

Always and always,
Yours
Clyde

SCHOOLBOY BLUES

I see the kid out of the corner of my eyes, like a phantom. He doesn't want to be here. He wants to be out kickin it. Over at Scottie's apartment. Drinking the fine. Snortin the positive. Getting loaded. But he's here, glassy eyed crying for help behind the wolfgrin and the rapid rap. He comes to school because it's his only link with something else and he doesn't know what that might be anymore. He comes closer, wide-eyed and wreaking of boo. He doesn't know what to do when I say his name. "Donnie. I need to talk to you."

He slows and I reach out to lead him out to the hallway. He yanks his arms up like he is about to pounce. The rest of the class goes into a hush.

There is only one thing to do when nothing comes to mind. Moo. I blow out the sound from the top of my palette. "Maaaooooooo!" Donnie freezes like he is being held up. Time beats in silence. The class comes unhinged. Amidst the laughter, Donnie's hands fall and he manages a smile. I call a break. The class slides outside and I look into his glassy eyes.

"I'd like to help you, Donnie. I know how you feel and I know you don't have to feel the way you do." He slumped and began to cry.

I worked with him and tried to stay with him for another semester, but the drama was real: his older brother was blown up in Iraq; he had no place to live; no transportation; no job; no parents (his mother was a meth head and his father, a raging alcoholic). He did respond to an internship as a sound mixer for a while, but soon sought out his old using buddies and was off to the races. Donnie died face down on a kitchen floor at 18, the needle still stuck in his arm.

Why have all these children come to us now? Where will they go when they're gone? Will they return? Will they have questions for us? Do we dare answer?

EIGHTEEN HUNDRED MILES OF ELBOW ROOM

(Being a dialogue between a father and his fifteen year old son, in the summer of 1997)

Tim:

Eighteen Hundred Miles of Elbow Room. I like to create titles! This one comes from an old 1930's tune called "Fifty Miles of Elbow Room" that I heard the other day on the radio by an obscure black anonymous choir. It's interesting how seeming random bits of information can weave together thoughts and ideas in ones mind. This old song has such vitality! It reminded me that most of our seeming obscurity is actually a benefit and allows us to be authentically creative, without worrying about anything else. I was also reminded of the idea of freedom and what that means to me. I know that the only real freedom for me is my own internal freedom, the infinite room of my spirit. So the freedom I have sought and yearned for all my life has always been there, although I often resisted feeling and exploring this freedom because of what I perceived were barriers to freedom in the world of other people, places and things. For me, freedom is my process of going through the mental barriers that prevent me from being fully alive, fully conscious of where I'm going and who I am. So, I need more than fifty miles of elbow room. I need eighteen hundred miles, so that I can really fly! Eighteen hundred miles is also the approximate length of this country's border with Mexico. The idea of a border also brings to mind other thoughts about freedom, its lengths and limits. Maybe I should increase my border size!

Josh:

Yes, the only real freedom is internal freedom, the infinite room of ones spirit and it's always been there! Chaos never died. The chains of law never existed. True freedom comes from embracing the notion that freedom is in your head. Even the oppressed slaves can be free. Everyone is free, for freedom is an illusion and is as prevalent as all other illusions. Why is it that one man can embrace the illusion of currency with passion, yet have no emotional attachment to the illusion of freedom? One man who knew that freedom, along with everything else, was Emperor Joshua Norton 1, Emperor of the United States and Protector of Mexico. Although a street vagrant, he wrote treatises that appeared in local papers, was given dignified clothes by local shops, and introduced a currency that was accepted by the public. So, by fathoming himself an emperor, Norton became one.

Tim:

Well, the only Norton I am familiar with is Ed Norton (Art Carney) of the old "Honeymooners" television series. I love the idea that someone can "fathom" himself! I would like to address the idea that everything is an illusion, another mental preference or belief or opinion. Is nothing real, then? I prefer (my opinion) to think that it is not all or nothing, that there is both the illusion and the reality. For me, real has to do with the unanswered and perhaps unanswerable mysteries of my soul, with all that inner searching and some kind of awareness of my own inner knowing that I can't quite describe. It is this knowing and the increasing awareness of this knowing that somehow makes me authentic and truly connects me to the seeming chaos and allusiveness of the world "out there." I do not have to know anymore how and why this is. I just allow myself the joy of dwelling on this and letting this thought guide me through the maze. All I do is come back to the peace inside my spirit and row my boat gently down the stream. So I don't worry much about the maya or the illusion, but I do enjoy participating in the drama of it all and striving to make use of my talents by following my intuitive, creative inclinations.

Josh:

Illusions are reality. Reality is an illusion. I'm the whole mind. I'm the mind's hole. Everything is true in some sense, false in some sense, meaningless in some sense, true and meaningless in some sense, false and meaningless in some sense, and also true, false and meaningless in some sense. This represents the one notion that I feel actually transcends the realm of that which can be spoken of and seemingly understood. This would make the paradox the one thing that actually exists (and therefore does not exist). The paradox, an infinite regress, is to me the one concrete thing in a world of illusions (or, if you prefer, reality), because it breaks both of these confinements. The paradox is reality and is illusion, therefore it is neither. Just as the holy man transcends the body, the paradox transcends the set of universal rules that have been falsely created, or, if not, it transcends the chaos that is in effect even before law is instilled. Even more than that, it does not recognize these things as more than what all else is. Everything is theory (this must be so because our perception is tainted by our senses, the things that allow us to perceive), thus everything is equally real or equally false. This shows that law and order, and reality and unreality are among all of the other sensationalized topical theories, subjective nonsense that passes for rational thought. Think of it this way: if everyone around you went crazy all of a sudden, you would be called the crazy one. Just remember: "Anything quoted is a lie."

Tim:

Ah! You have avoided my brief discussion about "knowingness," that has been a topic of discussion since the Tao, since Plato and even since Robert Anton Wilson! Everyone outside of me is crazy! So am I! It is in this mutuality of insanity that I must do my work and live this life, so my inner perceptions (not my profane judgments) lead me through the labyrinth of your paradox (Is the plural of paradox, paradise?). Although it keeps me crazy in some ways, all of the paradoxical ideas (e.g. you have to give it away to keep it; the sacred and the profane exist hand in hand, etc.) serve as a reminder of the great mystery of life and actually serve to bring me the peace I was talking about before, by urging me towards simplicity, creativity, balance and a continuing sense of wonder. So, the paradox, or the seemingly absurd or contradictory, is the fuel to my own invention. As the folk singer Kris Kristofferson once said, "I'm a walking contradiction, partly truth, partly fiction." Would you have me believe that my take on things is part of the sensationalized and subjective nonsense that passes for rational thought these days? I would argue that there is something behind my thought that is impervious to such a judgment, that there is a value and meaning and connection in my human beingness that transcends nonsense and impacts the whole. I am free to express myself in an ocean of possibilities. This is the hard part of this great big, happy, sad life, only because there seems to be so much resistance in the world out there and in the world of my own self centered ego that makes demands of my time, my thoughts, my emotions, my behavior and my relationships. My story continues to unfold into and through this resistance, always toward astonishment.

Josh:

Ones life can be looked at as a work of art. Anything that goes into it is necessary to the finished product. This makes everything inherently justified. So, all that one can strive for is to make of one's life the best art that they can make. This being known, one can live life free of preconceived conditions, only striving to achieve through their own evolving aesthetic. If you are satisfied with your life in the end, then it was a satisfying life, an obvious detail, but perhaps an overlooked one.

DIARY
SPRING 2000

(How the title of this book came to be)

I believe in miracles. I am 55. I turned pro less than a year ago, after I made my first hole in one and won $10,000. Why not? I can play a little. I am going to garner one of the four spots available in the Monday qualifier for the Las Vegas Senior Classic. I will win the tournament, outduelling Hale Irwin in Sudden Death. I will hole everything, drain that white ball right into the big black endless bottom of the cup.

The last and only time I played with Hale was at the Trans-Mississippi Amateur in Kansas City along about 1967. Hale Irwin, Sherman Fingers and Tim Flood. Quite a memorable threesome. Two of them now quite obscure. Sherman was a great player from U.S.C. Maybe he will show up as an aging rabbit like me, to try and beat Hale in the late afternoon of life. Hale was pure then, a real knife thrower. The only young guy around who was better was Johnny Miller, who was an absolute phenom. I didn't beat Hale that day in Kansas City, but I am going to take him down this week, in honor of my past – of a life half-squandered, like debris scattered old country road.

I peaked at 16. Club champion at Phoenix Country Club in 1962 (juniors were barred from playing in it after that). Made the sectional qualifier for the U.S. Open that same year. Flew up to Denver with Johnny Bulla. I was trying to become one of the youngest qualifiers ever, behind Nicklaus and Bobby Jones. Bulla was great. He told me all the old stories. How he piloted many of the pros around. How he once told Snead that he "couldn't play a lick." We played 36 holes in one day at Denver Country Club. I played with a guy named "Barbells Harry," from the Dakotas. I shot 146 and was low amateur and first alternate for the big show to be played at Oakmont. Got a U.S.G.A. medal, but no one withdrew from that Open. Bulla snapped his putter early in the first round and had to putt with his 2 iron. He shot 151 but laughed about it and told me many more stories on the flight back to Phoenix. I love his generation.

I remember following many Phoenix Opens in the late fifties and early sixties. I'd run around for ten hours a day at the tournament, following everybody. Littler, Ed and Marty Furgol, Stranahan, Souchak, Hogan, Snead, Paul Harney, Dutch Harrison, Terrible Tommy Bolt, January, Sifford, the Heberts, Chi Chi, Arnie, George Bayer and on and on. These guys were real characters, bigger than life. Bigger than life ended with that generation. I just want to be bigger than life this week in Vegas. Bigger than Hale.

Las Vegas. The fertile plain of vagueness and vacuousness. A monster wrapped up as a child's toy. The Stand. A fitting place for the end or for a new beginning, for the dream coming true. It's not that I'm taking this too seriously, just pushing for childhood's extension, like everybody else that's here. It won't be long now until that Monday rabbit starting time. Gentlmen start your engines. One hundred and fifty six players playing for four spots in the big tournament. All dreamers, just like me. Except I have the edge, a little tip from Johnny Boo Boo Bulla himself, recently unlodged from memory shards of that trip so long ago. Johnny said, "You gotta hit the ball with the right hand. Square, right down the line." So, I'm out of this faux motel, the Ballburst Hotel and Casino, and headed right on down the line.

First practice round at the TPC Canyons. I understand why the big old pros want to play the real tournament at TPC Summerlin. The Canyons has forced driver carries of over 240 yards, cliffs, washes and water. Design treachery. Anything off the grass is absolutely dead. Fast hard greens. Long. 7,200 yards. If the wind blows, even Lon Hinkle will be pressed to get it in under 80. Yea, Hinkle is in this Stormy Monday thing, along with 155 other assorted liver spotted wrinkled lip over-50 manboys. All are jonesin for the big show. For the chance to tee it up with Hale. You can't miss a shot if you wanna dance some more. As my sponsor, Paul Spankleton says, "Bury it!"

Second practice round. I'm hitting it good, trying to remember my swing thoughts from when I qualified on a Monday at age 19 to get into the Tucson Open. I watch the boys on the range. Big-wristed old touring pros, truck drivers, policemen, three teachers, rich and poor retirees, club pros, muni-hustlers. All the various hues and stripes of males cursed with the snake-bit golf obsession condition. All out here trying to analyze it, fix it, capture it, and get it on when the bell rings. I play with a pit boss from the Dunes, a recently retired fire chief from Tustin and a grizzled 66 year old club pro. All pros now because they paid their entry fee. All hunting Easter eggs. All slouching towards their private Bethlehem where only four of them will be born.

Ring! 7 A.M. tee time. Drew first off of the tee. I dreamt all night of how to get by the second hole! 196 yards into the wind and rising sun, downhill to a narrow green surrounded by a desert hill on the right and a deep arroyo of death on the left. After narrowly missing a 10 foot birdie on the first hole, I hit a solid 6 iron on the 2nd to a left rear pin position. I stobbed it, then left the 5 footer short, hanging on the front rim. Par. I was relieved, though, surely the next sixteen holes were to be mine!

They changed the tee on 3. Made it shorter, with no forced carry over the rocky barranca. I played safe with a 3 wood and drilled it down the middle, through the end of the fairway. The ball was in 4 inch grass on a downhill slope short of a cart path, 100 yards from the pin. I made the fatal error right there. I forgot to grip the wedge firmly. The pitch squirted straight right into a creosote bush in the desert. Shanks for the memories! The mutilated head trips began. Deep stuff percolating in my mind. Not as deep as the contemplation of a sex change operation, but deep enough. I crammed it out about 5 yards into some tall grass and then hit a good firm raking wedge that hit 10 yards short of the hole, did a drive by the pin and rolled right over the green and down an embankment. My flop shot went 10 feet past the hole. Left the putt short again. Triple bogey. My blood boiled and my cells percolated. This is what dying must feel like. I crushed my drive on the next hole, but pushed it right, over a mound and into a water hazard. Drop. Hit a 3 wood 255 yards just left of the par 5 green. Chipped up 2 feet short and made the putt for par the hard way. Charging for birdies, I three putted the next 3 holes for bogies. I was done. Put the fork in me. Dead man golfing. I managed to finish the round with a forced smile, but my soul was left back on number 3, smelling suspiciously like creosote after a rain. 82 strokes later I remembered what my sponsor had once said, "Golf is not a game of mercy."

I gunned my pickup down the road, glad that the stations of the cross were over, down towards the traffic jam at Hoover Dam, past Wikieup and Wickenburg, finding some solace in the fact that 152 other hacking pilgrims were in the process of doing the same thing, finding some joy in shots hit on the money, in the lessons learned, in the rounds yet to be played. I follow dreams of a ball in flight.

THE 12 STEPS OF GOLF

1. We are powerless over the flight of the ball and our game has become unimaginable.

2. We came to believe that a power greater than ourselves could restore us to our fantasy of hitting it dead solid perfect.

3. We became willing to turn our swing over to the PRO, as we understood him.

4. We became willing to undertake a thorough inventory of the defects of our swing thoughts, our thought swings.

5. We became willing to share these defects with ourselves, our PRO and our golf partners.

6. We became willing to have these whiffs removed.

7. Having asked for their removal, we agree to become teachable (or at least approachable).

8. We became willing to list all those people we have harmed - through errant shots, shouts and obscenities.

9. We made amends to all those we have hit, except when to do so would cause further harm.

10. We became willing to take a daily inventory of our swings and behavior, and when we were wrong, promptly took our penalty strokes, dropped another ball, and hit it again, smiling.

11. Sought through prayer, meditation, contemplation and various other means, to maintain conscious contact with the ball for as long as possible, down the line of flight.

12. Sought to refrain from carrying our concept of the game to others and to practice these principles in all of our matches, conceding to our innermost selves, that we are all "dogged victims of inexorable fate."

ACKNOWLEDGMENTS

A high school teacher of mine once referred to those who had peopled his life and disappeared as ghosts of the living. I have been fortunate to have had many guides in my life who have ferried me across many rivers. Some of them are no longer in my life, having moved on, passed on and otherwise disappeared from my scene. I am deeply indebted to all of these people: like Jan who let me live in the bow of his boat and pointed the way to the sea; Terry, who assured me that death is part of life and that a light awaits; Billie, who always said that she'd rather be out playing with the monkeys; Frank and Duke, guardian angels who still protect me. There are many more and I know that they are not really missing, that they are right here in my heart, like those who are with me and inspire me every day: my ever loving wife Tryshe, who shows me the true meaning of love; my sons, Josh and Gabe, who walk with me awhile on the journey and give me great insight and connection; my mom and dad, Marge and Clyde, gone, yet here, the best; my brothers and sister, Pat, Mike and Mimi, for all their love and support; my dear friend Pat, whom I have known for almost 50 years and who has provided an endless laugh and much food for expression in this book; my mentor, Gregge, who instills astonishment; and Craig, who understands the quagmire and is determined as I am to find a way out. This book is for all my family and friends with whom I have traveled. We all swim in the ocean together and ride the waves. We all follow dreams of a ball in flight.

www.ingramcontent.com/pod-product-compliance
Lightning Source LLC
Chambersburg PA
CBHW030521260626
47157CB00005B/1831